UNEEK

SONJA R. E. OMERZU

UNEEK

This is a work of fiction. Any characters, businesses, places, events, and incidents are either the products of the author's imagination or used
in a fictitious manner. Any resemblance to actual persons, living or dead,
or actual events is purely coincidental.

Printed in the United States of America

Hardcover ISBN: 978-1-959096-22-1
Paperback ISBN: 978-1-959096-23-8
Ebook ISBN: 978-1-959096-24-5

**Canoe Tree
Press**
4697 Main Street
Manchester Center, VT 05255
Canoe Tree Press is a division of DartFrog Books

I dedicate this book to my grandmother, Elsa Daudert, who always inspired me to reach for the stars. She taught me patience, love, consistency, and perseverance. An artist herself, she breathed the creative spirit into my soul, so I could develop the gifts God bestowed upon me at birth. Oma, as she was called, was the most influential and nurturing person in my life. I dedicate this book to you, because you dedicated yourself to me.

"Don't walk in front of me… I may not follow.
Don't walk behind me… I may not lead.
Walk beside me… just be my friend."
—Albert Camus

CONTENTS

PART 2

Part 3

PART 1

CHAPTER 1
UNEEK'S ORIGIN

In the eternal vastness of infinity, there existed a gargantuan, gorgeous nebula, inconspicuously tucked away in the far reaches of outer space. Thousands of light years in diameter, the nebula was basically a recycling center of cosmic debris. It was an immense dynamic conglomeration of cosmic clouds of dust and gases. The clouds were made up of the leftover material of supernovae, explosions of dying stars, colliding galaxies, and discharges from jets of rotating accretion discs surrounding black holes.

Powerful energy centers were dispersed throughout the nebula. These were the products of gravitational confluence of cool, cosmic dust and hot primal gases. As these massive energy centers grew denser and hotter, myriads of new stars and star clusters spewed forth like an enormous, pyrotechnic display. The beautiful, galactic garden spawned millions of stellar flowers which illuminated the entire nebula. Once expelled from their wombs, infant stars were held close by motherly gravitational pull so they could continue to grow and develop.

Having existed for billions of years, this spectacular, luminous phenomenon was well established and was known as the Esoterica Nebula. Not only the home of countless stars, but it was also the home and birthplace of Uneek.

CHAPTER 2
GETTING TO KNOW UNEEK

Uneek was extraordinarily unique. He was one of a kind. Nothing in the universe was quite like him. He in turn realized that each life form, each microscopic organism, every galaxy and heavenly body was unique, as well as every rock, mountain, river, and ocean. Each had its own particular story of survival. Each manifested itself in a universe of continuous change, occupying its own place in space and time. You are unique as well.

At birth, Uneek was simulated into a variable spark of energy, a star-like being. In some ways he was like a super intelligent humanoid inside a luminescent body. The capabilities and abilities of his mind had been forged from light, honed by millions of years of experience, learning, and development. He was acutely aware of his surroundings within the Esoterica Nebula as well as distant regions throughout the universe.

He didn't have a biological brain, but rather a highly active energy receptacle/transmitter system. He could absorb and emit immense amounts of telepathic energy and data. His mind eventually developed into a flowing current of truth. He grew to know and understand the intricacies as well as the vastness of the perplexing universe with its natural laws. He learned the how, what, where, when, and why things were the way they are.

His conception of emotions was beyond the realm of perception. It did not stem from a physiological expression of the mind or body. The revelations of truth that he experienced were spiritual in nature. He ascertained the underlying truth of emotions by discerning the quality and intensity of the light energy they emitted. Happiness was serenely bright and light. Love exuded the purest form of light energy, a bright white, illustriously vibrant. Dark emotions were very weak in light energy or were absolutely devoid of light altogether.

This is how Uneek realized the emotions of other life forms, by seeing their energy levels which were revealed in an internal light energy spectrum. Slowly he had become aware that everything had its own unique energy field, even rocks and crystalline minerals, and you.

CHAPTER 3
UNEEK'S MISSION TO EARTH

Uneek's light energy glowed bright with enthusiasm, as he ventured out on his own for the first time. He had just left his home, Esoterica, and was embarking on an initial solo mission - a mission to Earth. He had studied the Milky Way Galaxy in depth and the Sun System in particular. He was especially intrigued by life on planet Earth and the turbulent history of its formation. His curiosity peaked at the inference that Earth served as a sort of way station for numerous cosmic space travelers. He would have to be cautious and remain undetectable as he approached the Milky Way. Due to the presence of dangerous life forms in this part of the galaxy, he did not want to draw attention to himself for his own safety.

Further research indicated that numerous, highly advanced beings had been visiting Earth for a long time. Not all of them were benevolent beings, conducive to harmonic interstellar coexistence. Some were outright hostile and belligerent toward Earthlings as well as toward members of other intergalactic civilizations. They were unnatural, dark, and evil entities and could be deadly. Uneek needed not only to remain inconspicuous, but also, he didn't wish to cause any disruption in Earth's natural progression of life.

CHAPTER 4
ON HIS OWN

Uneek was cruising quietly through the universe, traveling at an incredible velocity many times the speed of light. His highly advanced civilization had attained faster than light speed travel ability after millions of years of technological research and development. It was the envy of many, lesser advanced interstellar civilizations. Esotericans had discovered how to harness dark energies and many other obscure force fields that existed within the dynamics of the nebula.

Uneek's ultimate mission was to ascertain and assess the problems facing Earthlings in their spiritual evolution and technological progression. For reasons yet unknown, Earthlings were lagging behind in their natural growth as a species. Their advancement seemed to be thwarted by globally oppressive forces that were destroying the unity of the species. They were still using antiquated systems to generate energy even though more advanced, higher efficient forms of energy were well known. Catastrophic, natural and unnatural disasters were beginning to occur more frequently. By now, Earthlings should have already been integrated into intergalactic affairs, commerce, and advanced space exploration. Overall, Earth beings were a worthy and viable species, but something was wrong, and Uneek wanted to find out what it was.

Uneek had been educated for many years in the overwhelming number of unique civilizations that existed in the multiverse and their individual stages of development. Uneek had finally reached a high level of proficiency and was now taking his first official

vacation. He had been on many previous training excursions throughout his area of the universe, but they were always conducted by teaching staff with chaperones. He was finally on his first journey to outer space all by himself. Any further education would be by his own preference, no longer guided by the Esoterica Council's teaching schedule. He was finally free to learn and explore as he wished. The future was his!

Glowing warmly, Uneek was delighted to be alone at last. He glanced over at a beautiful burst of stars, emulating from the center of an awe-inspiring, reddish pink nebula. It was immersed in a massive, bluish purple gaseous haze. Blue and yellow stars shot out like fireworks from the centers of massive energy dynamos. He savored the visual beauty of space as he passed by its many glorious manifestations. In particular, he was astonished at the breathtaking views of spiral galaxies with their sparkling, twinkling star systems. Spectacular visions of new galaxies forming from colliding galaxies whizzed by. Multicolored bands of spiraling cosmic clouds exhibiting innumerable, suspended stars fascinated him. He marveled at the awesome display of nebulae, quasars, neutron stars, and supernovas. Creation was an unbelievably beautiful work of art! The austere vastness of endless space lay before him, and he was finally free and at peace. The glorious radiance of heavenly bodies and worlds was a wonderful contrast against great expanses of stark blackness. The panorama of beauty gave him euphoric sensations, and his light flickered excitedly. He could live here forever!

Dimming with contentment, Uneek laid back and absorbed the beauty in his mind and spirit. How consoling it was just to be! At last, he was one with the universe!

Chapter 5
The Historical Archives of Earth

Shooting through space by light years, Uneek engaged the archives of Earth history and its origins. He didn't know why this knowledge pulled at his heart strings so strongly, but it drew his undivided attention. The story of Earth's continuous struggles to evolve viable life forms was absolutely fascinating to him. He began streaming.

Planet Earth had experienced tremendous global, geological changes in the past 5 billion years, as it took form and developed into the planet it was today. Most of the Earth's formative years occurred during the Archean Eon which lasted 3.5 billion years.

Primitive forms of life eventually came into being 2.5 billion years ago during the Proterozoic Era. Meteors, asteroids, and comets continuously pummeled the Earth, depositing bacteria into the primordial soup of prehistoric oceans and seas. Single-celled organisms began to grow, flourish, and proliferate.

Life slowly continued evolving for 300 million years throughout the Paleozoic Era. The oceans filled up with a wide variety of marine life, both flora and fauna. Life seemed to be well on its way evolving into new species and plant phyla. Then, 252 million years ago in the latter stage of the Paleozoic Era, during the Permian period, a catastrophic disaster befell Earth. A huge off-planet comet, asteroid, or meteor collided with Earth. The impact caused molten magma to erupt from deep within Earth, breaching the unstable crust and mantle. It rose up from underground forming super volcanoes in what is now Siberia. This was the beginning of the end of most life - the Great Permian Extinction.

An enormous cloud of volcanic ash, pulverized rock, and a toxic mixture of gases blasted up into the atmosphere, surrounding the entire planet. Volcanoes had expelled sulphuric dioxide, methane, carbon dioxide and numerous other toxic gases into the air. The ash cloud blocked the sunlight, vital for plant life and photosynthesis. A global winter followed which froze the planet. An ice age began.

The oceans acidified killing 95% of all life that had evolved for millions of years. The few surviving life forms struggled on, eventually repopulating the world with new plant and animal life forms. This extinction event marked the end of the Paleozoic Era and the beginning of the Mesozoic Era.

The Mesozoic Era consisted of 3 periods: the Triassic, Jurassic, and Cretaceous. As the ice melted, carbon dioxide levels were restored. The resurgence of life slowly emerged in the tropical ecosystems of the Triassic Period. An abundance of vegetation grew back along with the evolution of primitive animal life forms. Marine life had literally crawled out of the oceans to live on land. Life had evolved from astral bacteria to fish, and eventually to land animals - insects, reptiles, birds, and mammals. Lizards evolved in time to become larger and larger reptiles, which eventually led to the Age of Dinosaurs. They reigned supreme throughout the Jurassic Period until the end of the Cretaceous Period 66 million years ago when another catastrophic disaster occurred.

This time it came in the form of an enormous asteroid the size of a huge mountain. Traveling at approximately 40,000 miles per hour, it impacted Earth in the Gulf of Mexico. The massive impact shook the entire planet and caused Earth's atmosphere to reach temperatures close to 500 degrees Fahrenheit. 75% of all life that had taken millions of years to evolve was destroyed. The 175-million-year reign of the dinosaurs literally went up in flames and smoke. This extinction event marked the end of the Cretaceous Period in the Mesozoic Era.

Chapter 6
The Dream

Uneek abruptly stopped the stream of knowledge pouring forth from the archives. He had just experienced a strange sensation, a subliminal message. It toggled in his mind switching back and forth like a pendulum, pulling him from premonition to foreboding and back again. He couldn't comprehend its significance, and the uneasy sensation eventually dissipated. His inner light stopped fluttering.

Puzzled, he returned to the stream and went back over the feed. Once again, he felt the weird sensation at the exact point that told of the extinction of the dinosaurs. His curiosity peaked, but he still couldn't fathom its meaning. All he could conclude from this uncanny experience was that it signaled a warning about the future - a future with a strange connection to the past - specifically 66 million years ago! He had no clue beyond that what it meant. He was baffled and confused.

Continuing the feed, Uneek learned that this extinction began the Cenozoic Era. With the extinction of their primary predator, the dinosaurs, mammals finally emerged from their hiding places and evolved into what are now extinct primates, numerous types of hominids, and eventually modern-day Earthlings. Uneek was extremely surprised given Earth's past, that life even existed on Earth at all. He thought to himself with wonder at life's fortitude, its persistence, and determination to continue battling and struggling to exist against all odds. The story of life on Earth was absolutely miraculous. Each form of present-day life was a manifestation of an eternal past!

Later on, after Uneek had finished the overview, he had fallen into a deep sleep. Suddenly he found himself in the midst of an extraordinary dream of a strange, beautiful world. As the dream progressed, a breathtaking blue planet unfolded before him. The dream also revealed starving humanoids, abused animals, and the destruction of the planet's habitat and rain forests. Meanwhile, on the other side of the world the same human species were laughing hysterically, poodles were adorned with bows, horse hooves were carefully manicured, and verdant gardens and orchards were meticulously tended to. It soon became clear that this world was not only plagued by hunger and disunity, but also by disease, drought, and uncontrollable wildfires. Severe weather patterns were causing havoc across the world. All of this presented a peculiar dichotomy of existence - so much suffering occurring while others boated drunkenly around, throwing their empty beer cans in lakes, or cruised oceans in their exorbitant yachts.

Several figures of the dominant species inhabiting this world had attained worldwide control. They continued to encourage the usage of fossil fuels to produce energy, which in turn provided something called money. The air, water, and land masses were severely polluted with dangerous, toxic chemicals. All life forms on this world were subject to the by-products of industrial emissions. It was a world being destroyed by dominance, carelessness, ignorance, greed, and neglect. This was happening because of an insatiable appetite for power and control at the expense of their ecosystems along with all its life forms.

Uneek jolted awake when he realized that the planet was being destroyed by some of its own inhabitants! It was a horrifying prospect. Uneek abruptly flinched in astonishment, when he also realized that the inhabitants of this world were Earthlings and the world in his dream was Earth!

CHAPTER 7

DOUBTS

Uneek had been given the ability to redirect his itinerary at will as he made his way to Earth. This enabled him to visit interstellar phenomena such as star systems along the way. He thought about the places he would like to go and came up with some viable possibilities.

For now, he would just lay back, unwind, and enjoy the ride. It would be a while. It was a long way to the part of the universe where the Milky Way Galaxy existed.

Uneek listened to the Star Wars theme music as he glided along through an area of empty space. Star Wars was well known throughout the multiverse. It had been immediately disseminated everywhere by a multitude of space civilizations. The story was broadly accepted as an interesting depiction of an emerging primitive society. It presented a glimpse into the social, technological, and spiritual perspectives of Earthlings. It became a source of comedy for many advanced aliens, but Uneek did not find it humorous. Instead, he was even more interested in the spiritual and moral aspirations that some Earthlings possessed. He was fascinated by the ongoing battles between light and dark forces for control of their part of the universe. This was exactly why he was on his way to Earth. Uneek anticipated that a similar type of struggle was actually occurring there as well. He would learn more in real time.

The melodious vibrations of music were uplifting and comforting to him in his current state of solitude. His light energy dimmed in contentment as he reached into his mind for the list of places he might like to explore. A short excursion to a special place would be quite refreshing and serve to rejuvenate his waning impetus.

All the research he had done so far regarding the current situation on Earth had left him exhausted. The prospect of dealing with the massive problems facing Earthlings and having a positive impact on Earth's future made his mind reel in doubt and uncertainty. He questioned his ability to make a difference. He imagined he may be biting more than he could chew. He was traveling to Earth which may end up having even bigger problems that he had not foreseen and may not be able to handle. He could not possibly orchestrate a positive outcome for his mission to Earth on his own. He would be encountering forces much more powerful than his own. These forces were deeply ingrained physically and psychologically in the fabric of humanity. He was a mere light being functioning on a spiritual level. He would need help. But from where, from whom?

CHAPTER 8

CROSSROADS

Uneek minimized his energy to a dim glow, just a small pinprick spark of light, as he neared Crossroads. He had decided to visit the central logistical hub for cooperative, galactic commerce in this portion of the universe. The bustling hub was situated in an area of the cosmos composed of prolific cosmic phenomena and was surrounded by innumerable galaxies, looming, illustrious nebulae, and violently active quasars.

The actual hub was a huge artificial construct suspended in space near a binary star system. It was built by the harmonious collaboration of thousands of members of various galactic civilizations. It served as a meeting place to conduct galactic commerce, to share and obtain higher learning, and to deal with interstellar socio-political affairs.

Crossroads, as it was called, enabled advanced space civilizations to procure and barter for needed goods and natural resources. Esotericans were regular patrons of Crossroads and frequented the hub almost on a daily basis. Raw materials mined on asteroids in Esoterica were transported to the hub in exchange for other much needed, hard to find supplies and technical equipment.

Mining asteroids and uninhabitable planets were the main source of acquiring materials. The practice was widespread throughout the cosmos. It was the major activity for the extraction of pure elements, precious and semi-precious metals, valuable minerals, crystals and ores. Many materials, however, were produced or synthesized in laboratories making them even more valuable and expensive.

There was a constant flow of huge cargo transports and massive supply shipping lines entering and exiting the Crossroads complex. Many exited just as heavily laden with cargo as when they first arrived. Goods of every kind were up for grabs in exchange for the appropriate payment. The concentration of galactic commerce in Crossroads offered its customers the availability of almost every conceivable commodity, from medical, agricultural, industrial, construction, and fuel supplies to more personal items such as space suits and foodstuffs. Large transport vehicles as well as spaceships were also readily available, as were powerful energy producing systems, atmospheric regulators, and terra-farming equipment.

Advanced weapons systems, however, were strictly regulated by the heads of the commerce council division. Strict oversight was enacted in these types of sales to ensure their use would be for defensive, protective purposes only. Weapons were sold exclusively to entities of the most highly advanced, benevolent civilizations and required meeting extensive qualification standards.

Many hostile entities tried to infiltrate the restrictive, oversight apparatus in an attempt to obtain the most powerful, advanced weapon systems known. However, these attempts were always in vain when the buyers were subjected to truth detectors. These were psychological systems capable of discerning the true intentions of individuals. This verification system was similar to the one employed by Uneek with his ability to ascertain truth, and both analyzed light energy emissions. No infraction of the strict code of weapon procurement in the established commerce system had occurred since the deployment of this highly sophisticated technology. Nevertheless, this didn't deter hostile entities from trying. Any such successful sale was conducted under the table and offsite by hostile profiteers. These sales usually involved forms of technological, how-to knowledge, not the actual hardware.

Overall, whatever you wanted or needed, you could find it at Crossroads!

CHAPTER 9
THE LEARNING CENTER

An advanced center for higher learning had been established in Crossroads as well. It was administered and conducted on a voluntary basis and was staffed by the most highly evolved space beings in existence. Entry into the educational establishment was strictly guarded lest undesirable, hostile beings obtained access to secret knowledge of energy propulsion systems and development of dangerous weapons.

Uneek had visited the learning center before as a youngling on a "field trip" offered by his space school in Esoterica. He had been confined to the Center's public library along with his fellow school mates, teachers and chaperones. Uneek had found the entire experience totally unproductive and boring. He ended up getting in trouble, when he led a group of friends into a restricted area where the sign read "Learning Center Personnel Only".

Uneek was found to be the perpetrator of this aberrant disruption to the established curriculum and its schedule. A library security officer abruptly escorted Uneek to a private room, where he remained locked up for the duration of the field trip. He was forced to sit in front of a huge book entitled "The Philosophy of Ethics and Morals".

After being released from the room, he endured a host of belittling criticism, derogatory comments, and laughter as he rejoined the group to journey back to Esoterica. He could remember a classmate yelling at him, "You're weird, Uneek! You look weird, and you smell weird! 'Uneek, the Freak!'"

Inwardly, Uneek was smiling, because he hadn't read a single word of the ethics book. Instead, he focused on watching the constant flow of spaceships coming and going as they passed by the window. He spent the entire time fantasizing about what kinds of worlds they had come from. This was much more exciting to him than any other part of the field trip. He assured himself that in time, he would be free to explore the universe on his own, investigating other worlds and learning what he really wished to know. Uneek thought to himself and promised that one of these days in the future, he would return to Crossroads and visit the great commerce complex, watching the spaceships all day and all night long!

CHAPTER 10

RETURN

Uneek was here now at Crossroads once again. This time he was older, wiser, and free to pursue the knowledge he needed. He had to find possible sources of assistance in dealing with what he perceived would be a harrowing experience on Earth. He had a strange inkling that what he had learned so far about Earth would turn out to be only the tip of the iceberg. Instinctively, he foresaw a much graver reality than was depicted in his research of the archives. He had to prepare himself for the worst. He had a lot of homework left to do. He was determined to find answers no matter how long it took or where his search would lead him. Uneek's energy light glowed brightly with a heightened sense of commitment and determination. After considerable deliberation, Uneek chose to eventually make his way back to the Learning Center where he hoped to find solutions and some much-needed guidance. He had many, important questions that required answers to an extremely vital mission. But first, Uneek took a detour to visit the real-time dynamics of the bustling commerce system. This massive operation fascinated him. He had made numerous trips to much smaller supply depots around Esoterica, but to experience the operations of the mother of all hubs was the most exciting to him.

CHAPTER 11
EXPLORING CROSSROADS

Uneek's insatiable curiosity and love for learning led him to explore his surroundings. The magnificent Crossroads complex was composed of a variety of storage warehouses, each with specified loading and unloading portals. The portals were accessible directly from space so spaceships could easily enter and leave with their cargo. Landing docks were assigned to incoming customers, according to availability, arrival time, type of cargo, and spaceship size.

Each warehouse stored specific commodities. Some were designed for product preservation like nitrogen storage for sensitive electronic parts, while others were refrigerated for particular foodstuffs and medicines. Drop off portals for bulk, unspecified goods were available to sort the goods and redistribute them to specific storage units for resale.

An elaborate system was in place designed to manage all financial aspects of operations: order fulfillment; inventory management of all outgoing, incoming, and warehoused goods, and the functions of packaging, shipping, returns, and quality assessment. Most goods were readily available for immediate procurement on the spot.

As Uneek traveled through the complex, he marveled at its complexity and efficiency. He enthusiastically soaked up every detail like a loofa sponge. Crossroads was the largest, most automated, logistics system in the known universe.

Captivated by the vast variety of spaceships all around him, Uneek watched with fascination as they landed and took off. He wondered where they had come from, what type of propulsion system each ship had, and how fast it could travel. Uneek's curiosity peaked when he saw a huge, super ship slowly leaving a massive dock. As it rotated to face open space, the iridescent ship spanned the length of 10 or more regular-sized ships. It made no sound whatsoever as it suddenly disappeared, but not before revealing the ship's name displayed on its hull: *Excalibur*. It certainly lived up to its name, an entity of mysterious, magical power!

Having experienced the vast array of intergalactic transports from breathtaking, super ships to rickety, primitive ones absolutely unfit for traveling, Uneek was finally satisfied with his thorough perusal of the commerce aspect of Crossroads. Uneek slowly made his way back to the infamous Learning Center.

Chapter 12

The Amphitheater

Uneek floated through the towering metallic and crystalline halls of the Learning Center. He headed to where his childhood, private room was. Startled, he noticed that the architecture of this part of the center had changed dramatically. The infamous private room of his childhood visit was gone along with all the familiar adjacent rooms and structures. Now there existed a gigantic, amphitheater with walls that rose up opening to the celestial heavens. The perimeter was built in tiers to accommodate hundreds of beings. Astonished, Uneek noticed that each seat was currently occupied. And what was even more surprising, was the dead silence that permeated the entire amphitheater.

Uneek remained inconspicuously hidden behind a huge entrance pillar. Confused, he tried to catch his bearings. He cautiously took guarded peeks around the pillar to peer at the inanimate crowd. The audience consisted of representatives of every benevolent species in existence. It dawned on Uneek that he had somehow stumbled upon a meeting of great importance, and that the absolute silence was the sign of ultimate respect and solemn reverence.

Uneek looked up through the open aired ceiling into endless space. Seeing the beauty of the cosmos had an immediate calming effect on him. He searched his mind for an explanation, wondering how he happened to be here at this particular moment in time. He had entered the Learning Center with a past mind set, as a youngling searching for his private room. Somehow, he had inadvertently gained access through the security shielded entrance to the amphitheater. A rare occurrence of a dimensional time shift placed him here as his memory state faded and his present surroundings crystalized. During the shift he had become momentarily nonexistent, undetected with no identity signature. The black out had occurred simultaneously, as he had easily floated through the security identification check. Uneek mused in puzzlement exclaiming to himself, "Holy Quantum Leap!"

By an unexpected, enigmatic fluke, here he was in the midst of a very special proceeding. He had no clue just how special it was, but somehow, he had gained access to a secret meeting of the Celestial Council of Life!

CHAPTER 13
EYE OF THE NEEDLE

Uneek remained hidden behind the pillar. He wondered how much longer the audience would stay frozen in place and what was going to happen next. He suspected he was in for a lengthy, boring presentation about the current state of affairs of civilizations in the universe. To make things worse, there would probably be a long, drawn-out statistics report. This was the usual agenda of meetings he had previously attended in school. Uneek was not at all interested in listening to another tedious, formal speech.

He started, squirming restlessly behind the pillar and pondered how he could possibly escape the upcoming session. He couldn't think of any avenues of escaping indiscreetly. Every option he came up with would disturb the proceedings, drawing attention to himself. He would end up getting caught in the act and have hell to pay. He didn't know the penalties for a security breach, but he imagined the sentence would be stiff. In this particular case, the consequences could be quite dire. He'd probably end up in solitary confinement as a spy or worse! Uneek was definitely stuck. It looked like he would have to endure this dreadful, time-consuming event. He stopped fidgeting and resigned himself to the inevitable.

Once again, he peered at the audience when he suddenly felt a slight vibration coursing through him. It grew more apparent as it slowly intensified. Numerous, more powerful vibrations were now pulsating through him. Directly aimed at his mind, Uneek could only describe them as some sort of advanced electronic probe. He realized that it was focusing on the innermost depths of his soul.

The audience began to stir in their seats, and several actually stood up. They were all perceiving the same phenomenon! As the vibrations grew stronger delving deeper, Uneek became terrified. The core of his mind and soul was being exposed layer by layer. In some strange way the source of this frightening experience seemed strangely familiar! The probe gently made contact with his true being. Uneek froze! Suddenly, a dazzling ambient light filled his mind.

A group of lucid beings appeared in the midst of the amphitheater. The vibrations reverberated throughout the entire space. Slowly, Uneek began transcending. The physical reality of his surroundings faded away, disappearing into nothingness! He was gently lifted into another dimension, one of remarkable, ethereal beauty. Uneek floated further and further away as he moved into the mysterious realm. He dissolved into a state of aesthetic spirituality and was no longer visible.

Chapter 14

The Celestial Realm

Aghast, Uneek mused at the mystical realm of sheer beauty that lay before him. It was so exhilarating that if he had lungs, he would have lost his breath! The landscape filled his being with awe. Uneek had visited many interstellar worlds in his lifetime, but none compared to this! Majestic, translucent mountains rose so high that their peaks disappeared into the soft mist lingering in the sky. The brilliant heavens were illuminated in bright yellows and purplish reds resembling a huge, vivid fuchsia blossom. Millions of crystalline, water droplets were suspended in mid-air everywhere, glistening aquas and silver. Looking out across the realm's expanse, Uneek noticed areas where the sparkling particles shimmered gently downward in cascading, swirling spirals. Millions of droplets softly splashed down onto a chartreuse blanket of moss-like flora. Rays of diffused star light shone through the misty atmosphere, dappling the lands with a plethora of colors never seen before in any spectrum. The entire

realm exuded an ethereal ambience of harmonic peace and joy. This was a space in time that was indescribably exquisite. Uneek's spirit lifted beyond his usual state of euphoria, and his trembling soul surrendered humbly to this heavenly space.

Looking down, Uneek peered quizzically at distant stars twinkling through a deep, dark crevice in the ground. He pondered how these windows into alternate universes could possibly exist everywhere in this sublime realm.

Suddenly, he felt an eerie presence subtly approaching from behind him. He turned to look around barely able to discern a group of light beings lingering in the mist who had gathered close to him. The apparitions beckoned him to follow them, as they slowly retreated into mist. Uneek solemnly obeyed and followed in the direction in which they had disappeared. He was led to a clearing where an assemblage of ghostlike beings was suspended in mid-air, and he halted before them. He recognized some of them from the amphitheater.

An unseen source softly addressed Uneek speaking in a vibratory voice. "You have entered through the Eye of the Needle. Only the pure in heart and mind are able to enter. You are safe here, and we welcome you."

Uneek was momentarily astounded as explanations, instructions, and guidance flowed telepathically from an illusive entity. He carefully absorbed the information which was streaming directly into his mind. He didn't know what messages the others were receiving, nor did he know whether the others were aware of the messages transmitted to him. The communication that Uneek received explained that he had been selected by the Celestial Council of Life to appear here before them.

"We enabled you to pass undetected through the security veil at the Learning Center. The momentary space-time void you experienced was not a fortunate accident. It was orchestrated by us."

Uneek was amazed at this revelation, and he listened even more intently.

"We know of your intended journey to Earth. We need to provide you with extremely vital knowledge before you actually enter that part of the universe. It is meant to assist and protect you.

"You are a light being, an emissary of peace, hope, and truth. Because of your essence, we must warn you about those who would destroy you if they knew you were coming to Earth.

"Earth is one of many inhabited planets in the Milky Way Galaxy that has concerned us for a long time. A number of hostile interstellar beings have swarmed into this region of the cosmos raising havoc.

"A galactic battle has been raging between the forces of benevolent, harmonious beings and those of evil who have no regard for other life forms. We are actively involved in trying to maintain the well-being of these compromised planets. However, we remain indiscrete and unobtrusive lest we provoke the ire of the hostiles. Any overt action on our part could result in complete devastation of Earth. The collateral damage would be catastrophic. It has happened before in many other star systems.

"Throughout the millennia, we have continued to deploy emissaries to these endangered worlds as we have on Earth. We guide Earthlings so they can reach their destiny which is to join the rest of the benevolent space communities existing throughout the universe.

"There are a number of hostile civilizations from different galaxies who discovered Earth and its valuable resources. Their intention is absolute control of these worlds and all their intelligent life forms. They wish to exploit mineral wealth, develop a massive, interstellar labor force, and build the most powerful weapons in the universe. They have no regard for the well-being of Earth nor for its inhabitants."

Uneek sighed deeply and continued to listen.

"They have infiltrated the minds of Earthlings turning many into slaves of an oppressive hostile system. They have used unethical means to seduce the minds of Earthlings into believing in the hostile agenda.

"Their greatest passion is to be worshipped as the absolute, highest authority. They strike straight at the heart of human beings who seek self-validation and beseech a higher power of love, understanding, and hope. This is the exact point where masquerading hostiles step in to take advantage of naive Earthlings."

The message ceased momentarily for emphasis. Uneek's research and conclusions regarding Earth were confirmed by the Celestial Council of Life. Speculation about his worst fears had become the truth. Uneek soberly embraced the enormity of what had been revealed to him. His journey to Earth would not be the vacation he had been hoping for.

CHAPTER 15
THE ECLIPSE

The enormous Crossroads complex was situated at the edge of a binary star system. Lux and Pelia danced around each other in wide, elliptical orbits.

Selica, a huge, rocky planet, was held captive by the gravitational pull of the binary system and slowly orbited outside the stars' paths. Minimally affected by forces of the binary system, Crossroads maintained a relatively fixed location. Only an occasional adjustment was required using thrust jets to compensate for natural cosmic drift.

Selica's "weather" was in constant flux due to the proximity of either Lux or Pelia. There were long periods of unbearable heat and intense radiance whenever Lux or Pelia came near. Alternately, when the binary stars were distant, Selica fell into periodic deep freezes. It was inhospitable for Selica to support life with its unstable environment. However, during short periods of intermittent, moderate temperatures, Selica served as a suitable station for visitors. Crossroads used the planet as a storage site for larger starships, cargo, and transport ships which were too massive to store at the main complex.

Total solar eclipses involving Lux, Pelia, and Selica had occurred approximately every 1.2 million years. The alignment of the three celestial bodies cast a huge shadow on Crossroads plunging it into complete, frigid darkness for hours. This had only happened twice on Crossroads, since it was established 3. 6 million years ago. Now the time had come for such a total eclipse to occur and in only a few days.

Uneek reflected on some of the messages revealed to him by the Celestial Council of Life. He learned that Earthlings had to be extraordinarily astute to survive hostile invasions of their minds. In order to maintain natural freedom, humans had to remain completely focused on survival mode,

especially while sleeping when they were most vulnerable to mind invasion. This was a feat few Earthlings could muster. Most fell into the grips of hostile control.

The hostiles had deployed psychological warfare of epic proportions against humans. Most humans lived in carefree abandonment. Many preferred escaping reality and numbing their senses with the help of alcohol, drugs, sex, and living in fantasy worlds. Awakening to the truth resulted in a complete upheaval of their world with total paradigm shifts in their thinking and way of life. The hostiles knew that Earthlings had to remain happy to minimize any chance of insurrection. Keeping Earthlings naive and content, was the main goal of the hostiles.

The truth of the existence of extraterrestrials was not taught in educational or religious establishments on Earth. This knowledge was hidden from the public and considered absurd and crazy. Weren't humans the greatest creation in the universe? This belief was another ploy by the hostiles to ensure ignorance.

However, benevolent extraterrestrial contact was occurring on a wide scale around the globe. Neither the hostiles nor humans could control these contacts. The doors of truth were slowly opening, and hidden knowledge was becoming more and more prevalent. Humans were also discovering the truth found in surviving ancient texts and religious writings, most of which had been torched! Humans were defying what they were being taught, stepping out of the brainwashing curriculum. More and more, they were delving into the taboos, the realities of hidden knowledge.

Uneek had to remain vigilant. The gravity of the facts was more intense than he had originally imagined. His existence would be in jeopardy if the hostiles found out he was coming to Earth. They would annihilate him if they had the chance. Afterall, he was a light being, the direct antithesis of everything the hostiles stood for. Earth was beautiful. Nature was sacred. Life was a gift. These manifestations of reality would prevail over the ugliness created by evil. Uneek's faith, understanding, and awareness was stronger than ever. He was bathed in sacred enlightenment, and it shone ever more brilliantly, like the star he was. He was ready to tackle all adversity that the universe revealed. He had no fear, only love and spiritual harmony which emanated from the depths of his soul.

All of a sudden, the entire realm shuttered with a jolt.

Chapter 16
The Attack

The mysterious jolt was subtle as it rippled through the realm. Nothing had really changed, but an eerie silence fell upon everyone. The Celestial Council had all but disappeared leaving only two members to handle the continuing affairs of the meeting. Immediately they addressed the group with reassurances of their safety concerns. The group was told that the Council had left to investigate the situation outside of the realm. They were told to remain calm. Updates would be transmitted as information streamed in. It was suggested that each attendee meet and introduce themselves to their assigned mentors.

Uneek's mentors were a group of representatives from the Pleiades, the Seven Sisters. Being close at hand, the Sisters beckoned for him to join them. He mingled easily among the Sisters sharing in mutual, congenial conversations as they awaited word from the Council.

Information slowly trickled in with alarming news. Crossroads had been attacked at the exact moment that the total eclipse had occurred.

Crossroads lay in complete darkness. In a series of garbled, broken transmissions, they were told, "Much damage… many lost… Learning Center gone… beginning to get cold, no lights… no power… no systems operating… Complex totally disabled. Stay put until we return. You are safe in the realm."

At the onset of the eclipse, hostile forces had invaded Crossroads, putting into action a meticulously planned attack. Inconspicuously, the hostiles had infiltrated the loading docks, the supply bays, and landing pads. What seemed to be a normal day of business, the complex was unusually busy conducting commerce. The supply facility bustled with heightened activity as cargo transports and freighters surrounded the entire complex, waiting their turn to land.

The hostiles swarmed in at the precise moment of darkness. They had enveloped the entire facility in an ultrasonic field immobilizing and destroying all personnel. Unsuspecting and unprepared, logistics personnel were easily overcome with lethal sonic charges. Never before in 3.6 million years had the center been attacked in such a massive, aggressive way. Previous attempts were limited to trivial smuggling rings which had always failed. The hostiles' well-coordinated plan enabled them to immediately incapacitate the emergency systems that were designed to provide light and heat to the complex during the eclipse. The entire energy grid was destroyed with powerful electromagnetic pulse (EMP) weaponry. The destruction of the grid rendered Crossroads completely defenseless and vulnerable. In a matter of seconds it was transformed into a dark, lifeless, dysfunctional entity, completely isolated from the rest of the universe.

The hostiles easily accessed the towers housing the control panels. They were destroyed on the spot with EMP blasts ensuring that all existing operating functionality and communication capability were knocked out forever. Crossroads customers who had gotten caught up in the chaos of combat and who survived the initial onslaught were rounded up and held hostage. They could possibly be used in future negotiation as leverage. Incoming and outgoing spaceships and cargo transports were confiscated when possible or vaporized as a last resort.

Prior to the invasion, a large convoy of hostile forces had been deployed to raid Selica. Having synchronized all attack actions, the hostiles had stealthily approached and invaded Selica in one deadly sweep. In just a few minutes, they made off with the spaceships of their dreams! They disappeared into the cosmos to reconcile with the rest of the Crossroads invaders later. The hostile forces left Selica in their newly acquired fleet and retreated to the predetermined, rendezvous point in deep space that would be close to impossible to find. They had hollowed out a gigantic, remote asteroid and equipped it with living quarters, space portals, and huge storage areas.

The hostiles at Crossroads quickly filled their transport ships with powerful armaments, state of the art energy systems, and the rarest of raw materials. Using their highly advanced, materiel handling equipment, they levitated the booty onto the ships with ease.

The invasions of Selica and Crossroads were completed within 17 minutes! It had been efficiently and effectively executed by the most devious beings in the universe. Their payload was an arsenal of space vehicles and weapons which would allow them to build one of the most powerful fleets in the cosmos!

The last hostile transport left the skeletal remains of the complex to join the rest of their forces at the asteroid base. It served as a perfect camouflage to hide out in. The hostiles triumphantly rejoiced with pride at their bountiful acquisition, like fledglings marveling at their new, flight feathers.

Pelia emerged slowly from behind Selica. Brilliant, silver rays of Pelian starlight struck the frozen layers of thick ice that had completely covered the damaged structure. The glistening shell of what was once Crossroads was hurled into space. With no one left at the helm, it was ejected from the star system to wander aimlessly in the expanse of endless cosmos.

CHAPTER 17
UNWAVERING DEDICATION

After a lengthy absence, the Celestial Council of Life returned. Somber and shock-stricken, the Council members shared what they had experienced.

"Crossroads is no more. The largest and most sophisticated supply system that was ever constructed in the universe is no more. Completely destroyed and gone forever.

"The attack was swift. The losses are staggering. The most advanced spaceships ever constructed, and the highest technological weaponry are now in the hands of hostile sub-civilizations.

"They have made a mockery of benevolent civilizations and our virtuous purpose in life. The hostiles are not civilized entities. They are uncivilized sub-beings of darkness and death.

"Now with the destruction of Crossroads and the confiscation of its most valuable commodities, the hostiles will become more powerful than ever. They represent the greatest threat to life and beings throughout the galactic cosmos.

"Never before has such a travesty occurred. Such powerful spaceships and weapons in the hands of evil beings!"

Uneek, surrounded by the Sisters of the Pleiades, ventured to speak, but remained reverently silent. He nodded when one of the sisters poked at him encouraging him to speak up. He had spent time with the sisters getting to know them better as he had been directed to do. Electra was the one goading him, as Maia giggled from behind.

Alcyone turned to glare at Maia. She didn't believe it was appropriate to giggle given the dire situation that was confronting them. Her glare said it all, and Maia's light reddened. Uneek felt that he and the Sisters had become friends in the short time he had spent with them. They were all a quite jovial bunch of stars. Now however, was not the time for humor.

Uneek mustered up enough nerve to eventually ask the Celestial Council a question or two. "So, the Learning Center was completely destroyed. The hostiles stole high tech vehicles and weapons. My first concern is whether or not they gained access to the secret knowledge stored in the Learning Center? Secret knowledge of the most highly advanced nature technologies, theories, and the most recent discoveries in harnessing energies including those of dark energy. This knowledge was stringently guarded by the most advanced security systems known so it would never fall into the wrong hands.

"My second concern is this. Was the secret knowledge of highest sensitivity secured before the invasion and destruction of the Learning Center?" Uneek and the others waited with nervous anticipation for the response.

The mysterious, vibratory tone of the unknown, illusive being began to telepathically enter his mind giving him a message which only he could comprehend.

"The entire Learning Center was destroyed along with all its contents, books, journals, archives, and all electronic and crystalline stored material, both public and secret," replied one member of the Council. "It was all vaporized by the hostiles."

The crowd sighed with great relief. Knowing that the hostiles had not gotten their hands on any of this information was encouraging. It was gone forever, reduced to dust.

However, the answers that Uneek had telepathically received from the illusive being were different.

CHAPTER 18

AFTERMATH

The Celestial Council of Life wrapped up the meeting hastily stating, "The extent of our need to continue the concerted efforts to maintain peace and harmony in the universe has been drastically increased as a result of the successful hostile attack. We must vigilantly investigate all hostile affairs. We must discover their home base and any future plans of hostile intentions.

"Continue on your current missions. Coordinate with your assigned mentors for guidance and support. The natural guardian of the universe, Gaia, is also always available to assist you in any way she is able. She is a treasure trove of knowledge. Reach out for her if you find yourselves in trouble or need answers to questions of an important nature.

"Our work has become more dangerous, but also more vital to the continued preservation of interstellar life. Stay alert and aware of all things that cross your paths. We will contact you again in the future when such contact is warranted.

"Each of you can exit the realm by your own will power. Merely rise up beyond the atmospheric mists, and you will be returned safely to discreet locations where you will be able to resume your previous itineraries.

"Thank you for your reverent participation and dedication. Each of you is a light being of extraordinary caliber. We will prevail. We are the protectors of all life and nature. Nature is the precious essence of creation. We are counting on you and your continued support of life everywhere. It is the sacred way. Nothing can control it, conquer it, or obliterate it forever even though we have our setbacks. Creation declares the freedom of life and its divine right to exist and flourish. Remember always what stirs inside your hearts and souls and what you stand for.

"This meeting of the Celestial Council of Life is adjourned. Stay safe, go in peace, and shine on."

Uneek returned to the Seven Sisters. They enthusiastically bonded even tighter with Uneek since a deeper sense of spiritual purpose had been sparked in them. The closing words of the Council had an extraordinary effect of spiritual cohesion and reasserted their ultimate purpose.

The Sisters told Uneek that they were there for him if and whenever he needed them. "We have your back. Come visit the Pleiades sometime. You are always welcome, and we will embrace your presence. We will always answer your calls. Remember also to contact our dear friend Mother Gaia. We love her. Be careful during your visit to Earth. It is not exactly the most hospitable planet. Beware of hostile aliens and hostile Earthlings as well."

With that said, Maia chimed in, "Parting is such sweet sorrow", quoting Shakespeare's Juliet and giggling to herself.

As Uneek rose up into the mists, he heard the beautiful, melodious singing of the Sisters, a true, celestial choir. They vibrated in perfect harmony sending him off with a special farewell song. The song resonated within his heart and soul, and he would never forget the beautiful tune. Somehow, it came to be permanently imprinted in his mind.

Leaving the celestial realm as he rose beyond the mists above the mountains, Uneek found himself back at the exact location where he had originally veered off course for a quick excursion to Crossroads. He immediately transmitted a message back to Esoterica explaining what had happened, and that he was once again on his way. Uneek settled back and resumed his travels at break-neck speed to make up for time he had lost during the disparaging stopover.

Uneek felt fatigued and overwhelmed. He minimized and fell into a deep sleep quietly humming the Pleiadian song to himself until all went silent. He traveled through large expanses of space in this manner. He passed by innumerable galaxies and the immense, dark areas in between. When his being finally felt rejuvenated and adequately rested, he was signaled to wake. Checking his location, he was surprised by the distance he had traversed while sleeping. He was entering the quadrant of space where galaxies were spiraling all around him, galaxies including Andromeda and the Milky Way!

He had slept suspended in a trance-like state for a long time, covering billions of light years through space time. He was close to the outermost regions of space where he would eventually reach Earth. He reduced his speed and cruised slower. This gave him more time to rethink and process past events. He prepared for his arrival to Earth which was closer at hand than he expected.

CHAPTER 19
GETTING CLOSER TO EARTH

Uneek spent the rest of his travel time prioritizing the various aspects in preparation for the upcoming Earth landing. Recent events had taught him more than any book learning ever could. Experience was the best teacher.

Uneek relaxed, letting his mind wander. The last message received from the illusive being came to mind.

"Yes. The deepest and most sacred secrets had always been secure. The Learning Center never actually held this knowledge to begin with as rumor had it. The little bit of knowledge kept there had only been a superficial collection of vague, modern discoveries. The actual details were closely guarded and hidden. Only the archives of ancient writings provided in-depth historical data, most of which was ancient and antiquated. It was useless for development of modern high-tech armament. True, sacred knowledge was hidden in an undisclosed mental and spiritual realm only accessible by channeling.

"These secret records were not manifested in any physical reality. Rather everything was spontaneously captured by the universal consciousness, which is a compendium of life, the ultimate reservoir of all knowledge."

The illusive being found it unnecessary to divulge the truth to the rest of the assembly. For the sake of simplicity, it was easier and safer to believe that it was all destroyed. The rumors would spread, and the hunt would finally cease. The records never existed in the context that they were imagined anyway. The whole matter was quelled by circumstance and silence.

Why Uneek received the truth, he did not know. Uneek, however, knew and understood the existence of the Akashic records. He had accessed them in past channeling episodes. He wondered whether this was why he was told. Uneek was beginning to realize that there were many more questions being generated than answers coming in.

Now, however, Uneek had to concentrate on the main objective of carrying out his mission. Sometimes he wished that this adventure was just a pleasure trip, the vacation of his dreams. He was still so young. Life was exciting, and he wanted to enjoy it and not be burdened by the constant awareness of evil and evildoers. His recent experiences at Crossroads had so vividly impressed this truth upon him.

Suddenly an alert sounded in his mind advising him that he was approaching the Andromeda Galaxy, only 2.5 million light years from Earth.

Uneek checked all the criteria that needed attention before actually landing on this new, strange world called Earth. His ultimate purpose was beginning to develop into a daunting prospect. To comfort his weary mind, he hummed the beautiful Pleiadian song to himself. It worked and brought peace back to him.

First, he minimized himself further. Once he passed the moon, he would minimize to a tiny spark. He checked the appropriate time for entry in accordance with Earth's rotation, gravitational, and magnetic factors. He ensured that the integrity of all his programmed functionality and capabilities were intact. Next, he would find a safe landing site. Having gathered all the necessary data and studied the maps, he determined that the landing site should be somewhere on the coastline of the Atlantic Ocean. He reduced his speed to synchronize with the coordinates of his navigation system.

He planned to land on the dark side of Earth at midnight when human activity was minimal. He would recalculate a more exact landing spot as he descended through Earth's atmosphere.

Uneek transmitted a short report to the Esoterica Command Center. To guard against detection, he sent his message using an alternative energy system that would appear as normal Earth static.

Having completed all items on his checklist, Uneek concentrated on the view of Earth by engaging the telescopic eye in his mind. He was close enough now to pinpoint his exact landing spot.

As he passed the Earth's only moon, Uneek focused in on a remote area close to the shore of an immense body of water. As he viewed the vicinity, he saw a tall lighthouse. Uneek increased the power of the scope and saw that the lighthouse was perched on top of a rocky cliff. Several other cliffs rose up from a narrow-recessed inlet.

The entire area seemed to be uninhabited by humans. The lighthouse was old and seemed to be abandoned. Uneek chose to land near a large, nearby forest. He input the scope's readings of this location into the navigator and set the trajectory of his descent.

CHAPTER 20

THE LANDING

Uneek circled the Earth until he reached the side shrouded in darkness. Small specks of distant lights appeared everywhere below him and were highly concentrated in specific areas. Uneek realized these were the towns and cities of the Earthlings. He wanted to stay far away from them.

Uneek slowly descended through the atmosphere, until he perceived a coastline which divided a great land mass and an enormous expanse of water. As he descended further, he spotted the lighthouse in an area of cliffs along the shore. He floated downward softly landing on the ground.

He immediately took cover in a forest nearby. Making his way through the towering vegetation, Uneek paused to sit down below a blooming magnolia tree, its sweet fragrance permeating the night air. Uneek apprehensively peered around at the looming darkness. Eerie shadows danced mysteriously in the depths of the forest. In the dimly lit haze caused by his small spark, he could barely see the outlines of strange objects moving between the trees and bushes. His insides were reeling with a mixture of excitement, uncertainty, and anxiety. He had never felt this unsettled. He had to regain his composure.

Uneek activated his night vision function and looked slowly around again. In this awesome, alien world all forms of life were suddenly exposed in the dark recesses of the woods. Life was teeming everywhere. He had never been alone on an alien world. He had always been with a group of students accompanied by teaching guides and scouts while on exploration field trips to familiar planets.

He could have sworn that he noticed several sets of glowing eyes, peering at him from the darkness. Strange sounds came forth from the air, trees, and forest floor. Occasional chirps, a series of low, disapproving growls, and constant buzzing, clicking noises entered his auditory channels. His system identified them as a variety of birds, insects, and mammals. He heard the pitter-patter of tiny feet scampering away in all directions. He was amused by the abundance of active, nocturnal lifeforms.

The raw nature of Earth was wildly intriguing. This initial encounter with life on Earth was mysteriously beautiful and comforting to him. Fireflies flickered on and off all around him like tiny stars. Uneek's sense of peace and calmness spread gently throughout his being. As cumulus clouds moved across the dark sky, an occasional opening revealed glimpses of outer space filled with stars. Fully exposed, the full moon bathed the forest floor in soft, dappled patches of light. Shadows deepened as the trees and leaves were lit up. The contrast was beautiful. Uneek heard distant howling, closer growling, and flapping of winged creatures as they rose and flew away.

Uneek thought about his experiences at Crossroads. If it wasn't for the safety of the celestial realm, he most assuredly would have been terminated during the destruction of the facility. Uneek felt humbly thankful and incredibly gracious to be alive. He wouldn't be here now if events had taken a different turn.

Uneek was suddenly surprised by a deep-seated realization. The Sisters made him feel warm and cozy. Also, he had recently sensed fear, worry, and uncertainty. Was he actually feeling emotions for the first time in his life?

As he was settling in for the night under the fragrant, magnolia tree, he heard low, prolonged tones of agony reverberating from far off in the distance. Zeroing in on the direction of the sounds, he realized they were coming from the cliffs where the lighthouse stood. They sounded extremely painful and lonely. As the wailing continued, Uneek felt the desperation, the misery. Uneek accessed his sound decipher. The sad cries were unmistakably prehistoric!

Part 2

Chapter 21

Dawn of a New Day

The Sun star was rising slowly on the eastern horizon. Sunlight began filtering through the forest casting long shadows behind the trees. Wildlife rustled and songbirds called to each other. They signaled the beginning of a new day on Earth.

Uneek stirred from a long, peaceful sleep. Before he dimmed out during the wee hours of the morning, Uneek had reflected on his long journey here. He could have traveled to Earth much faster but had decided to take the scenic route. He thought about the flood of emotions awakening unexpectedly inside himself. He wasn't prepared to cope with these new emotions of fear, worry, uncertainty, and love? He questioned their timing, existence, and meaning. He had learned about emotions and knew that there were many different variations of love. The only form of love he had ever experienced was the highest spiritual, universal type of love or agape love. But what he felt with the Seven Sisters was different. It was warm and endearing, more like philia love that exists between friends. He would have to get used to feeling emotions and learn what to do about them. For now, he left them alone and safely hidden deep inside. He fell asleep content with his decision and the relative silence. The distant howling had finally ceased for the night.

As his drowsiness fell away from him, and his being lit back up, Uneek recalled the desperate cries in the middle of the night. "Prehistoric" was the analysis he had received from his acoustic identifier. Hundreds of images of prehistoric animals flashed across his mind, but he couldn't figure out which one he had heard. The cacophony of howling cries was so distorted by emotional distress that the exact species couldn't come through clearly. All he knew was that the wailing emanated from something huge. His curiosity got the best of him, and he floated up from where he lay at the base of the magnolia tree. He drifted slowly through the muggy, saline air in the direction of the lighthouse to investigate.

Chapter 22
Thunder Spotted

Uneek hovered above the abandoned lighthouse located on the precipice of the highest cliff and looked down across the Atlantic Ocean. A salty, warm breeze blew in from the east. The emergence of the Earth star blinded him as he faced the wind, pungent with the smell of marine life. The sun cast brilliant rays of light across the gentle waves below making them appear pink and deep blue as they undulated.

Catching his bearings, he floated down next to the base of the lighthouse. Uneek noticed he was surrounded by a semicircle of high cliffs. In its center was a small cove coming in from the ocean. The breaking waves dissipated as they entered the inlet lapping gently against the rocks.

Temporarily lost in the rhythm of the ocean waves, Uneek suddenly heard something below him. Listening intently, he heard snorting and baying. Then, he spotted it!

A huge mass appeared halfway submerged in the warm, shallow waters of the ocean close to the mouth of the cove. Using his enhanced ocular and depth measurement functions, Uneek figured the ocean was only about 25 to 30 feet deep where the mass was. Being half submerged, the animal's back was close to 50 feet in height at its shoulders! Returning to his ocular function, Uneek focused in and once again perused the "prehistoric" species catalogue in his mind. A match became apparent immediately identifying it as a huge, prehistoric creature called an apatosaurus! It was not supposed to be alive. Only the bones of these prehistoric animals had ever been discovered in excavations of the western part of this continent. They were carbon dated all the way back to 66 million years ago and earlier!

Uneek floated excitedly down the side of the cliff to the edge of the water. He was apprehensive and a little unsure about what to do next. He lingered on the beach as the creature dipped in and out of the water. Uttering prolonged, deep moans of pleasure, it moved slowly around as it bathed. What better time to go investigate a little closer while it was in a good mood. Uneek waited. He named the creature Thunder after its distant cousin, the brontosaurus or thunder lizard.

Chapter 23
Meeting Thunder

Thunder had been taking sun baths for several days, and Uneek watched him curiously and very carefully. He researched whatever he could find out about dinosaurs and their natural habitats during the evenings. All records indicated that apatosauruses were basically benevolent herbivores unless provoked. Then they could turn into a formidable force using their powerful tails as whips.

One night while resting underneath the magnolia tree, Uneek remembered the mysterious dream he had shortly after leaving Esoterica. This creature could very well be the one that the dream spoke to him about. His kind lived during the Mesozoic Era during the late Jurassic and early Cretaceous periods - 150 million years ago! The dream was telling him something about the Cretaceous period, but he couldn't figure out what it was alluding to. This must have been it. What was a prehistoric reptile doing here? It was definitely existing out of its normal Earth time.

Uneek went back to the shore the next morning and wanted to finally make contact. After a long, restless wait, the creature showed up late in the morning when the sun was high in the sky. As usual, it lumbered around in the tepid, salty water seemingly content and happy. His long tail smacked against the surface of the water causing huge splashes and waves.

Uneek cautiously made his way out to the creature whose head was now completely submerged. Floating in mid-air 50 feet above the waves, Uneek kept a safe distance as he patiently waited.

Suddenly with eyes closed, Thunder's head rose up from the depths of the ocean, and he snorted extra forcefully. A massive amount of briny water and phlegm was propelled from his nostrils hitting Uneek with full force. He was blown backwards 35 feet! Uneek screamed out loud as the thick, viscous substance sizzled and popped. Uneek wasn't hurt, just unpleasantly surprised.

Hearing the chaos, Thunder immediately opened his eyes and stared in disbelief at Uneek surrounded in steaming smoke. He was stunned at the close proximity of Uneek. Thunder snorted again, clearing out his enormous nasal passages. Not reacting in any other way, Thunder dipped his neck and head under the water again. After a few moments Thunder came back up for air and snorted again. Uneek stayed a safe distance away. Thunder was enjoying his sinus cleansing process, but before he had a chance to go under again, Uneek yelled, "Hey you! Aren't you even going to acknowledge me and apologize!"

Thunder was taken aback but only mumbled something under his breath.

"My name is Uneek. Who are you? I know you are an apatosaurus, but where did you come from and how can you be here?"

Thunder's eyes grew wide with astonishment, and he stared at Uneek suspiciously. Thunder froze in awe, and his questioning expression revealed intense curiosity.

Uneek repeated, "An apology? Can you hear me? Can you understand me?" He was speaking in the universal language that all life forms could understand, but he wasn't getting any reaction from Thunder.

Uneek continued, "I heard you howling last night, and I came here to investigate. You sounded so lonely and pained, completely opposite from the jovial time you are having now. I named you Thunder. Is that okay with you?" Thunder lowered his head and muttered to himself.

Uneek asked, "What did you say? I can't hear you."

"Thunder IS my name. I haven't heard my name spoken in such a long time, that I almost forgot what it was. You made me remember. How did you know my name?"

"I didn't. I named you Thunder after your cousin the brontosaurus, the 'thunder lizard'. It's a long story," Uneek said. "How did you get here?"

Thunder replied quietly, "It's a long story, a very long story."

CHAPTER 24

A FRIENDSHIP BLOSSOMS

The next few weeks were spent together learning about each other. Uneek had followed Thunder to his temporary resting place, a patch of land slightly elevated above the beach surrounded by lush vegetation. Uneek's magnolia camp by the forest was inaccessible, because it was too high for him. His monstrous, body mass made it difficult enough to get around on flat land, let alone climbing cliffs.

Impossible!

Their days were spent on the beach in deep conversations about where they were from and what they wanted to do.

Thunder told Uneek that he didn't know where he came from or what his goals were. He explained that he had been wandering around aimlessly for as long as he could remember, not knowing where he was and with no particular destination in mind. As long as the climate was warm and had plenty to eat, it didn't seem to bother him.

Uneek asked, "Why were you moaning so loudly in the middle of the night? You seem to be quite a carefree, cheerful fellow, especially when you're splashing around in the ocean."

Avoiding the question, Thunder replied, "The buoyancy that the ocean provides relieves the aches and pains in my legs. Besides, it reminds me of the basins my family and I used to wade in." He abruptly went silent, a distressed look on his face like he was trying to hold back tears.

After a long pause, he went on, "I miss my soulmate, Ella, and my young ones. I mourn for them at night. I cry for the life we had. It was paradise. I cry for my herd. I cry for all who perished. This world is a crap-shoot dichotomy of pleasure and pain, life and death. You never know what to expect next. The great wisdom of the mysterious Tao."

Uneek had studied the early writings of Lao Tzu and Taoism. He thought about the perfect balance of opposites in nature which was depicted by the pagua symbol, the yin and the yang.

This was what Thunder referred to. Apparently, he had also read Lao Tzu's philosophical writings about the true nature of not only the dynamics of planet Earth, but also the entire nature of the universe.

However, Uneek's mind was filled with questions regarding Thunder's past and current existence. Uneek respectfully kept them to himself. Little did he know that Thunder's mind overflowed with questions, too.

Thunder quickly changed the subject and asked, "What are your goals?"

Uneek briefly told him about his journey to Earth and his mission to protect all life. He included a short description of what had transpired at Crossroads and the ominous perpetrators.

Thunder immediately chimed in, "I've seen the spaceships of other worldly entities many times. They've been here for a long time. I saw them once with my family and many times thereafter. They seemed quite benevolent, but there are always some bad apples on every apple tree."

"You know what, Thunder? Something tells me we are going to become good friends. We can help each other. You are so knowledgeable and can teach me so much. With you by my side, I won't have to interact directly with Earthlings or the ETs. I can learn from you. I know I have a lot to share, also, and I can help you in return. We are both alone in this world, but we can be friends coexisting in a mutually supportive way."

Thunder replied, "I haven't been able to actually communicate with anyone for ages. I don't know why, but I prefer being alone. It's almost like I'm invisible to the world, but you can see me, and I do enjoy our talks. You are different, Uneek. You are very interesting, and yes, I do believe being friends with you will do me a lot of good.

I suffer from depression, anger, and loneliness. You help make the world a happier place. I know Ella would have liked you, too. You are definitely unique. Imagine that! My very own star friend!"

Uneek was glad that their relationship was growing amicably. However, he was deeply concerned about Thunder.

Something was wrong, very wrong. He would go back to the magnolia tree and do more research to find out whatever he could.

It was close to midnight, and the waning moon was high in the dark sky. Uneek turned to Thunder, "Hope you get a good night's sleep. See you in the morning."

Before he left, Thunder looked at Uneek and said, "I apologize."

"For what?", Uneek asked.

"For the nasal discharge I accidentally blasted at you. I just thought you were an oversized, common Lampyridae, a firefly, or as some call them, a lightning bug. I didn't think twice about blowing you away. I'm sorry."

Uneek replied, "Apology accepted. It really woke me up. I was sizzling and popping like water in hot oil. I screamed, because it caught me totally off guard. It didn't really hurt. It just startled the crap out of me. Never experienced an apatosaurus snort mucous at me before. It's okay, Thunder. I understand the circumstances. It's really kind of funny."

Thunder chuckled to himself and said, "Thanks. I know that if you weren't such a nice star, you could have blown me out of the universe!"

Uneek was amused at the visual he suddenly had watching Thunder blown to oblivion. Uneek definitely had the capability, but he had never used his power in that way. The bulk of his essence existed in an adjacent dimension. Just a tiny part peeked into this world's dimension, and only as a spark.

Giggling, they both bid each other good night.

CHAPTER 25

MAGNOLIAS

A powerful storm raged through the area that night. The winds blew ferociously, and the rain came down like a tropical monsoon. Lightning flashed brilliantly across the sky lighting up the entire countryside. Loud rumbles of thunder immediately followed. The lightning strikes were too close for comfort. Trembling with fear, the animals in the forest took shelter.

Uneek worried about Thunder. He did not hear any distressed howling that night, only the crashing lightning strikes, as they hit the highest pf objects. One of the enormous tentacles of electrical energy hit something in the distance with such force that the air rippled and the ground shook. The smell of smoke lingered in the air long after silence and complete darkness returned. The storm finally subsided.

Uneek stayed awake long after the tumultuous weather phenomenon was gone. He returned to his research, intent on learning more about Thunder's origins. He revisited the story of the huge asteroid that had collided with Earth in the Yucatan region 66 million years ago, resulting in the massive extinction of life around the globe. This was the exact time period that Thunder would have existed. Along with most plants and animals of the time, dinosaurs also became extinct. Was this the disaster that was causing Thunder so much stress? Did he somehow survive? He must have, because he was here now and still alive.

It finally dawned on Uneek where and when Thunder came from, and he understood Thunder's grief and sadness. He had lost everything.

Uneek was relieved that he wouldn't have to confront Thunder directly with some of his questions. He had figured this much out on his own. He also realized that Thunder had created a mental block to shield himself from the emotional pain that the past caused him. However, the main question still lingering in his mind was how he could be here now in this space and time? The whole unlikely scenario baffled him, and he fell deep asleep in a mysterious quagmire of possible explanations. Humming the song of the Seven Sisters brought him the solace he needed as he drifted off in a peaceful state.

The lightning storm had left a path of destruction discernable in the dawn's early light. A strong smell of smoke permeated the balmy, morning air. Waking later than usual, Uneek looked around at the fallen trees, large limbs, and magnolia flowers strewn around everywhere. The animals had returned to investigate, busily sniffing at the debris in search of something to eat. Songbirds happily tweeted their own particular calls, hoping to attract an amorous mate.

Accessing the archives again, Uneek read that magnolia trees had survived Earth's many cataclysms, continuing to evolve from prehistoric times over 100 million years ago. They exemplified fortitude, dignity, honor and respect. These attributes reminded Uneek of Thunder, who also exhibited these same traits. He had survived through the ever-changing ages with grace and a sense of stability.

Uneek picked up a large branch that had broken off from his magnolia tree. It was still covered with white blossoms. He left his resting place to present this ancient prize to Thunder and headed for the beach.

CHAPTER 26

THUNDER BEGINS TO OPEN UP

On his way to visit Thunder, the smell of smoke intensified. Uneek suddenly stopped to peer at the smoldering, charred remains of what was once the abandoned lighthouse. He recalled the crash of lightning and thunder from the night before. It was the loudest of any other, and he knew this huge strike had hit and destroyed the lighthouse, setting the wooden insides aflame. Only a partial stone shell remained still standing among the smoldering embers. He hurried along to the beach area to see if Thunder was okay.

As usual, Uneek found him floating around in the ocean frolicking in the warm waves. His tail was joyfully smacking at the surface, as he repeatedly dove under and back up. Holding the limb from quite a distance away, Uneek was happy to see Thunder emerge again, snorting and carrying on in extreme merriment.

Uneek yelled out, "Good morning. I have something for you!"

Thunder immediately waded to shore, waddling up the beach to meet up with Uneek.

"Good morning to you, too. Did you see that remarkable light show last night? I stayed up watching as the lighthouse burned. It went up like a tinderbox!"

Uneek answered, "Yes. Oh, what a night! Are you alright? I was worried about you."

Thunder replied enthusiastically, "Best show I've seen in years! I see you made it through. You should have joined me on the beach. We could have watched the fireworks together!"

Uneek added, "Without popcorn? I don't think so. Besides, I had other things to do."

Thunder looked curiously at Uneek and asked, "What are you holding behind your back?"

"Oh, just a little something I found. Here.", he pulled forward the limb and waved it back and forth across Thunder's nostrils.

Thunder's eyes grew wide, and his nostrils flared at the fragrance. "Magnolias! My all time favorite!" Thunder opened his mouth, grabbing the limb and stripping all the flowers off of it. He tossed the naked limb aside. "This is absolutely delicious! I didn't discover them until I moved here from out west." He chewed up the mouthful of blooms along with a couple of beach stones.

"Out west? When were you out west? That is a long way from here," Uneek questioned.

"I don't remember. I just know there weren't magnolia trees where I came from."

Laughing, Uneek said, "Magnolia's have medicinal benefits, too. They help with runny noses."

After lunch, Uneek asked Thunder to share more about himself and what he knew about humans. He didn't realize he had opened the door to Thunder's incessant rampage of rambling. Like releasing the cap from a pressurized container, Thunder exploded with knowledge that had been pent up inside him for millions of years. It was not entirely shared in an objective manner. Most was tainted with subjectivity and disdain. He had never had anyone to share with before. Now, all of a sudden, Uneek became Thunder's sounding board. Thunder's recollections and opinions poured forth with relentless attitude and impunity.

CHAPTER 27
THUNDER'S WORLD

Thunder was a little reluctant to talk about the times he came from. He had forgotten how to communicate with others and had only talked to himself. It wasn't until a lot of prodding and reassurances from Uneek, that Thunder finally started telling his story. The defining catalyst was Uneek's sincere interest and eagerness to know more about his story. That in itself gave Thunder all the impetus he needed.

Thunder asked Uneek, "May I start with a short, partial account of prehistoric Earth evolution before my time? Are you interested?"

Uneek gladly responded, "Oh, yes please. I want to learn as much as I can. Thank you!"

So, Thunder began. "The landscape of Earth was changing 252 million years ago. The great continent of Pangaea broke apart resulting in the continents we have today.

"There had been other super land masses in the past that had also broken apart and moved, not only Pangaea.

Turbulent, subterranean, tectonic plate shifts had changed the face of Earth. On land and under the seas and oceans, new mountain ranges and islands emerged. Magma constantly rose from the depths of Earth, spawning violent, erupting volcanoes. Earthquakes signaled ongoing plate movements and collisions. Whole worlds with their entire habitats disappeared under water and underground in massive, catastrophic subduction events.

As evidenced by the moon's numerous craters, impacts were plentiful on Earth, also. The Earth was continually bombarded by huge, incoming asteroids, meteors, and comets which added to the chaotic struggle for survival. Most of these exoplanetary bodies burned up upon entering Earth's atmosphere, but the larger ones made it through causing devastating impacts. It was a crap shoot of existing in the wrong place at the wrong time or just happening to live in the right place at the right time. Survivors evolved into what are present day life forms. Most plants and animals existing in the past are no longer seen on Earth today. They almost all became extinct. "

Thunder continued, "I came from a different place in time on planet Earth than what it is today. I lived in the Jurassic Period during the Mesozoic Era. The climate was a tropical paradise, hot and humid - the ideal ecosystem for all forms of life to thrive in.

"Mammals were low on the totem pole trying their best to survive in a hostile world of gigantic reptiles. They spent much of their time scurrying around and hiding underground and in treetops. Along with birds, insects, and diversified marine life, they continued to proliferate despite periodic devastation. Everything grew to abundance, and so did we, the monster lizards who sat upon the throne of world domination."

Thunder went on to further describe the ecosystem. "Huge ferns, cycads, fruit and nut trees, conifers, and a myriad of other unique vegetation grew plentifully. There was always plenty to eat. These were the foodstuffs of omnivores and herbivores, like me. Magnolia and palmetto trees flourished and originated during these times, too.

"Foliage, however, was not the food desired by carnivores. Many theropods were voracious meat eaters. They were feared by all animals, even each other. During the severity of numerous ice ages and years of darkness, many animals had turned to eating each other due to the scarcity and at times total lack of plant life.

"Tyrannosaurus Rexes were the most ferocious meat eaters, the kings of the dinosaurs, I could hold my own against them, though! Remind me to tell you the story about my most heroic encounter with one of them."

Thunder looked over at Uneek and asked, "Should I go on or have I lost you to boredom?"

"Please go on. This is fascinating to me! I'm not bored at all. It is awesome to be listening to a story of an actual descendent of these prehistoric creatures. And in person! Please continue!"

Thunder nodded.

"For millions of years, Earth was a dynamic, evolving world of continuous catastrophe, extinctions, and regrowth. This was the unstable, precarious world that I am originally from, and that we all live in today as well. I lived happily in this world before I was snatched from it. Snatched from my home, my family, and my friends. How this happened to me is beyond my comprehension. This is the exact cause of most of my stress - not knowing why or by whom, how, or what happened."

Exhausted, Thunder said to Uneek, "I'm tired and need to relax before evening comes. Please excuse me, but I'm going for a long float while the water is warm, and the sun is still shining.

I will tell you about my victorious, valiant battle with the T-Rex tomorrow. I am done for today and need some mental health nurturing. I hope you don't mind. We can continue tomorrow or the next day if you don't mind."

With that said, Thunder hoisted his body up, turned, and headed for the ocean. Hiding a hint of unexpected disappointment, Uneek responded to Thunder, "Sure. See you in the morning. Have a good night." Thunder just grunted as he lethargically entered the water. He was apparently dismayed at his past and present predicament.

Uneek was determined to try and solve Thunder's problem, but he didn't know how or where to start looking for answers. Then it suddenly dawned on him! The Seven Sisters had mentioned Mother Nature, Gaia, and told him that if he ever needed help, she would be there for him. He floated up from the beach and headed back to the magnolia tree. Helping Thunder had suddenly become his most important mission. He knew what he had to do - find Gaia. He started humming the sisters' soothing song. It filled him with hope and faith. He WOULD find the answers. At least he had ascertained the most favorable path that lay before him.

CHAPTER 28
DINOSAUR WARS

The next day at mid-morning, Uneek met up with Thunder again, who seemed rested and in good spirits. After a fulfilling breakfast and a pleasurable dip in the ocean, Thunder came to shore upon seeing his friend. Uneek reminded Thunder about the great battle he had mentioned the day before. It didn't take much pleading to get Thunder started. He puffed himself up and eagerly responded to Uneek's request.

Thunder began, "Tyrannosaurus Rexes or T-Rexes, prevalent in dinosaur habitats, were one of the most vicious carnivores in existence in prehistoric times. T-Rexes and other huge carnivores posed the biggest threat to the survival of brontosauruses, apatosauruses, and the myriad of other herbaceous quadrupeds existing at that time.

"Constantly monitoring my surroundings, we would submerge ourselves in swamp basins, whenever T-Rexes were spotted in the vicinity. This deflected attention by hiding our massive, enticing bodies as far underwater as possible and remaining as still as possible.

"If attacked, our whipping tails had the power to inflict death blows or permanently disabling wounds, and the threat vanquished. Many times, the tables were turned, and the injured carnivores became the prey to other hungry, carnivorous theropods

"Often, giant herbivores fell victim to the powerful, snapping jaws of T-Rexes, with jaw-filled, glistening, spiked teeth, two to three feet long. In one vulnerable moment, they could lunge at their prey, tearing the small head of an apatosaurus or brontosaurus completely off, crushing and swallowing it whole.

"If their heads were inaccessible, T-Rexes tore ferociously at their long necks, ripping out huge chunks of its soft tissue. The mortally wounded creatures writhed helplessly on the ground shrieking in excruciating pain, gasping as their tails whipped and lashed out in vain. They were slowly eaten alive. Lying motionless, the desperate flopping and rolling having come to an end, their roars of agony ceased.

"Within minutes a chaotic feeding frenzy ensued lasting for weeks, as famished carnivores of all shapes and sizes ventured to partake in the spoils. They feasted on the 15-ton carcasses, satiating their hunger, eating in turn according to the natural pecking order.

"The whip-like snapping sounds of apatosaurus' tails could be heard from miles away. The sound frequencies could reach up to 200 decibels, equivalent to the thunderous booms of modern-day fireworks. The piercing sound served as a warning to others that danger was near. "

Thunder recalled such a fearful encounter and began his personal story that he had promised to tell Uneek.

"My family, friends, and I were lazily basking in the warmth of the prehistoric, tropical sun, enjoying the temperate coolness of surrounding basins.

Suddenly, we heard distant cracks of snapping tails, the well-known sounds of distress, emanating from fellow quadrupeds. Alert with fearful anticipation, I felt the ground begin to tremble and saw ripples spread across the water basins. Immediately, I became suspicious of the possibility of impending danger and ordered everyone to remain submerged and to be silent. Even the littlest ones instinctually obeyed.

"Within a few moments, the largest T-Rex that I had ever seen emerged from the thicket of the jungle. It peered rapidly from left to right and roared so loudly that the trees shook. He spotted me when I came out of the basin and served myself up as a lure to deflect the T-Rex's attention away from the others. The T-Rex ran swiftly toward me. Knowing the T-Rex wouldn't enter the water, I turned my body around so my hind side faced the fast, approaching, furious T-Rex. In this position, my tail became my reliable weapon, while my head and neck were safely protected from the point of attack. As the T-Rex quickly closed the gap, I turned my head around to peer directly at the encroaching beast. With a heightened sense of acuity, determination, and courage that I had never felt before, my tail whipped rhythmically snapping louder and louder with focused precision.

"The T-Rex let out a deafening roar as it charged forward. The end of my tail snapped with a powerful strike at the face of the T-Rex! It was a direct hit at its snapping jaws! His head was instantly severed from its thick neck which burst open in a torrent of blood! The force of the blow sent mandible and maxilla jaw bones, skull bones, neck bones, teeth, and flesh spewing through the air in all directions. The T-Rex screeched from what was left of the stump of his throat. Gurgling sounds emanated from its bloody windpipe as it tried in vain to suck in air. It whirled around crashing to the ground with one last, agonized gasp.

"Awe-struck and in shock,

surrounding quadrupeds looked on as the headless T-Rex writhed and reeled in the mud, until it lay completely still. My family, and the others slowly began wading through the waters as far away from the dead T-Rex as possible. As we retreated, we joined together in a low, guttural song of contentment and relief. A deep, vibratory tone resonated throughout the land. Being the largest and most cunning of my kind, I became known as the 'Deceptive Warrior' by all whom I had saved. Word spread throughout our world, and a huge movement began to take shape. Everyone started whipping their tails at makeshift targets perfecting their skills. If we could possibly prevent it, never again would another apatosaurus perish in a ferocious, carnivore attack. We grew into a defensive army, and not another T-Rex ventured near our territory for years! We were slow and cumbersome, but we were mighty and deadly."

Thunder beamed with pride, and he eventually abandoned his euphoric memories to return to present time. He looked at Uneek for a response. Uneek was flabbergasted and exclaimed loudly, "Wow! What a story! What a tale of primal survival!"

Thunder smiled reassuringly at Uneek and said, "Pretty spectacular, huh?"

Uneek replied, "I know you are a very special apatosaurus, one of a kind, and I also know you are ready for a dip in the ocean. I have some things to talk to you about, but it can wait until tomorrow. I'll leave you now."

Thunder nodded in agreement, and Uneek watched as Thunder made his way back to his favorite water spot. Uneek giggled to himself as Thunder exhibited an extra swagger to his gait from his hind end, head held high, tail slowly swaying from side to side behind him.

CHAPTER 29
UNEEK'S PLAN

After leaving Thunder in his palmetto-lined, ocean front paradise, Uneek returned to his own temporary paradise in the magnolia grove. Comfortably settling in for the rest of the day, Uneek pondered over the next step in his itinerary. He and Thunder had to make their way westward. Winter would arrive in several months according to Earth time, and being a reptile, Thunder had to move to a warmer climate. Besides, Uneek needed to reach out and find Gaia somewhere along the way.

Uneek consulted Earth's GPS and studied the geographical coordinates and the options it presented. After great scrutiny, he decided to initially head northwest to Tennessee. Thunder would be able to maneuver over foothills, through mountain valleys, and follow river systems quite easily. Nevertheless, it would be slow going, since Thunder's top speed was roughly 20 miles a day, and that was on level ground. With all the detours along the way, circumventing high mountain peaks and narrow passages, Uneek calculated that it would take them about two to three months. He realized that this journey was vital in his search for Gaia. His goal was not only to obtain her expertise on how to free Thunder from his prison, but he also wanted to discuss another situation with her. He needed her help and guidance about a much greater, intergalactic threat. The hostiles were hiding somewhere in the vast universe with a growing arsenal of ships and weapons, no doubt recruiting other like-minded, evil intelligences. The search for Gaia was twofold and needed to happen soon.

Before he left the grove to tell Thunder about his plan, Uneek sent a message to his star friends, the Pleiadians, for assistance. As he was sending his message, Uneek noticed that a swarm of ladybugs approached and danced playfully in the air around him. Watching them with joyful amusement, he was surprised to see that each ladybug had seven spots!

Existing closer to the Milky Way Galaxy's center, the star cluster of the Seven Sisters was only a little over 444 light years away. It wouldn't take long to hear back from them. He needed more precise guidance in finding Gaia. With the communication transmitted, carefully and securely, Uneek left the grove, plan in mind. Even though dusk was beginning to fall, Uneek ventured back to the beach to speak to Thunder again before the end of the day.

Uneek found him napping under a group of palmetto trees. Thunder sounded like he was seriously in need of a bi-pap machine. He was sound asleep in a deep state of absolute relaxation. He was totally lost to the world around him, as powerful discharges of air bursting from his lungs made the palmetto leaves rustle like in a windstorm. Vibrations shook the ground, the trees, and nothing dared to come near, not even the ladybugs which had followed Uneek. In this supine state of oblivion, it would be difficult to rally Thunder enough to gain his undivided attention and listen to his plan. Uneek hated to disturb Thunder, because he really needed his rest. But his plan was just as important, and Thunder needed to know as soon as possible.

Uneek grabbed one of the fallen magnolia branches he had brought with him for Thunder's culinary pleasure and extended it toward Thunder. Uneek tried to position it under his nose, but when Thunder exhaled, the branch went flying through the air landing 20 feet away. That idea wasn't going to work. He would have to be quick. Grabbing a second flower-covered branch from the pile, Uneek waited and timed his approach more accurately. After all the air was dispelled from Thunder's lungs, Uneek stuck the branch in front of Thunder's wide nostrils again. As he inhaled, like a vacuum, he suddenly sucked the end of the magnolia branch right into his right nostril! Thunder momentarily stopped breathing altogether as the branch hung, dangling from his nose. Then an intensely loud, violent sneeze erupted sending flowers, twigs, and nasal fluids everywhere. He opened his eyes and glared at Uneek. "What are you doing?" he blurted out in anger.

Uneek replied matter-of-factly, "Waking you up! We need to talk. It's important."

Thunder snorted and said, "You could have just given me a gentle nudge or shook me a little!"

Uneek explained, "Trust me. That wouldn't have worked. You were so deep asleep, snoring like a freight train."

"Trust you? After sticking a branch up my nose?", Thunder retorted in disgust.

Uneek couldn't possibly explain further, since Thunder was totally unaware of his snoring problem. So, Uneek just asked, "Are you awake now?"

"Well, yeah. Unless this is a bad dream."

"Okay. Let's find a good spot to talk. How about that sand dune over there?"

Thunder reluctantly stood up, shaking his head and slowly followed Uneek up the large dune. Once seated, Uneek told Thunder of his plan, accentuating the fact that winter was coming. "We need to leave soon and get on our way."

Thunder replied emphatically, "I go to Florida for the winter each year! Why in the world should I go with you to wherever you're going?"

Uneek explained that they had to find Gaia. He finally let it all out. "There is something seriously wrong with you, Thunder. Uh, what I mean is you shouldn't be here. I don't mean you personally. What I want to say is that you shouldn't be here in this time and space. I want to help you, but we need Gaia to help us, too."

Pointing up at the darkening sky, Uneek said, "I sent for help from my friends, the Seven Sisters, in the Taurus Constellation. It is about 250,000 times the distance from the North American Nebula that you see above us. It's not dark enough yet to see the Pleiadian star cluster, but it's there," Uneek explained, pointing to the east of Orion's belt.

Uneek had finally gained Thunder's full attention, as he stared into space in wonderment. Thunder looked at Uneek and said, "Something is wrong with me, I know. I haven't seen any members of my own kind for so long. I'm isolated and alone, all alone. That is not right. I can see your kind twinkling up there all over the sky. Thousands of you! Why don't I ever see any of my own kind?"

Uneek felt a pang of sadness, and said, "That is exactly what we need to find out, buddy. We will wait to hear from the sisters, then we will look for Gaia. She will help us. Is my plan agreeable to you, Thunder?"

Thunder had tears in his eyes as he answered, "Yes, it is. I want to see my kind again. I miss them all, especially Ella, and my children, Harold and Patty. Yes! I remember their names! Those are the names of my children! Harry and Patty.

Uneek quietly left Thunder, who was now completely engrossed in a sudden host of new recollections and forgotten memories.

Chapter 30
The Trek West Begins

In the next couple of weeks, Thunder's memory was becoming more and more astute, as he remembered eons of experiences and knowledge that had blurred over time. His mind was clearing as was evidenced by a wide variety of talking points and intriguing topics during conversations with Uneek. His depression and self-pity were gradually subsiding and gave way to greater recall. Uneek benefitted immensely from Thunder's recollections. Much of Thunder's knowledge was attained from reading books, not just thousands of books, but millions of books. Other parts of his knowledge were gleaned while watching Earthlings and overhearing their secretive conversations. This was only possible due to the fact that his presence was unknown and unseen while in their midst. Thunder's invisibility enabled him to eavesdrop while only a few feet away. It was very easy for him to simply lower his massive head next to humans talking to each other. He had to be completely still and hold his breath.

Thunder became a storehouse of knowledge about human life, thoughts, emotions, and intentions. He also had a wealth of knowledge of manmade systems, the world order, philosophy, psychology, science, and nature. Sharing his vast knowledge, gave Uneek the extensive education he needed. This way he was able to learn much faster and in greater detail than if he tried to learn on his own.

Up until now, only Uneek could actually see Thunder, because he was multidimensional, and Thunder existed outside of normal dimensions.

Thunder's mind had frozen up in a rusty vice, and his spirit suffered from depression. All that was needed to free him from the downward spiral of mental destruction was a little oil and conversation. Uneek was that oil, the catalyst that got the wheels in Thunder's mind turning again and restoring the fluidity of his thought processes.

The quick response from the Seven Sisters was graciously received. The message contained vital instructions. "You will find a village of native humans who will guide you to Mother Gaia. Your instincts were correct, Uneek. Follow your itinerary as planned. It will lead you where you need to go. Speak to the village wise man. He knows. Good luck! We love you, friend. We will come to Earth one day to visit you. They included an audio of the sisters' songs before the communication came to an end. They had received no updates on the hostile situation as of yet.

Immediately, Uneek told Thunder, and their departure from the East coast would begin the very next day. It took 107 Earth days for Uneek and Thunder to travel to the land of Tennessee. They journeyed through the Appalachian Mountains which was the most time consuming and arduous for Thunder. They had traversed away from the coastal region into the foothills quite easily. Their itinerary took them through the most remote areas that Uneek could find. He spent hours meticulously researching the terrain ahead. They avoided cities and towns, discreetly remaining in uninhabited natural regions. Lakes and rivers were plentiful, and Thunder loved to indulge in them.

When they reached the Blue Ridge Mountain Range in the northern part of South Carolina, however, the going began to get more difficult.

Upon reaching the mountains, Uneek realized that ascending the mountains would be slower than he expected, and some were virtually impossible for Thunder to climb. Several peaks rose to heights of over 5,000 feet and were covered in ice and snow. Many days were spent traveling around them, backtracking at times, in order to find more suitable passageways. They reached many dead ends along the way and had to retrace their steps. Uneek searched for alternate routes that Thunder could manage. Uneek scouted constantly, hovering above the landscape, and tried his hardest to find ways through valleys, up and down riverbeds, and hillsides hidden between the mountains. Uneek had to consider Thunder's tremendous size and weight, as well as the angles of slopes, both ascending and descending. He measured the width of narrow passageways

through mountain gaps and riverbeds, and the stability of the ground. In this way they inched forward. Thunder was feeling the painful effects of this difficult journey, both in his legs and in his feet, which began to blister and bleed. His toenails were worn down to the bone. He began losing weight, despite the abundance of vegetation and water that he consumed. Nightfall brought a biting chill to the air, and Uneek built campfires at every stop. As daily temperatures rose, Thunder relished in the warmth of the summer sun blanketing his back.

Thunder required a lot of rest in order to keep up with such a demanding schedule. He also had to soak his sore feet and body frequently. Completely exhausted and withering, Thunder finally placed one of his huge, heavy, front feet on the ground in the land of Tennessee!

That evening Uneek and Thunder were glad to finally relax around the warm campfire. Thunder was exhausted and thankful for the much-needed reprieve from the grueling day's walk. After a smaller than usual snack of berry bushes and a long, satisfying drink of fresh water from a nearby creek, Thunder instantly fell into a deep sleep.

Uneek stayed awake long afterward. He was relieved that Thunder had made it this far, but also realized he was in pretty bad shape. He decided that they would spend several weeks in this area to give Thunder time to recuperate before continuing. Uneek reflected on their accomplishments thus far and the upcoming challenges they had yet to face. The message from the Seven Sisters was reassuring. It provided him the hope and faith he needed to continue with optimism. Traveling alone would have been fast and easy. But with an apatosaurus as a traveling companion, it was quite a challenging ordeal and required the greatest of patience. At least they were on the right track. They would find the Wise One and Gaia. They would confront whatever else the future had in store for them head on.

Finally feeling confident and comfortable, Uneek minimized. He needed to wind down from the harrowing journey, too. Half asleep, he was abruptly awoken by an incoming alert. It was an important message from the Celestial Council of Life. The message came in as a continuous stream of data that entered his mind in rapid succession. It was accompanied by a series of electronic sounding beeps. Momentarily alarmed at the transmission, Uneek started deciphering the secret message.

"Warning! Warning! We have been alerted that the hostile forces have reemerged from their hiding place. They have splintered into several factions and are headed to numerous areas in the cosmos. They are on the attack. The presence of one faction has been detected in your sector. Outer space surveillance teams have reported that they have attacked a benevolent civilization approximately 312 million light years from Earth's Sun star. They ravaged the planets and killed millions of the inhabitants. They did not attack the Lucien system for weapons, for there were none to be had. They are using the outer planets and moons as bases to establish a stronghold. The few Luciens that survived were transported to a moon of one of the inner planets. Their home planet was destroyed, propelling it into their system's star, Lucia. They are currently retrofitting the captured Lucien starships into weaponized warships. The four outer planets in the system are occupied by the hostiles.

Our friends, the Luciens, have been virtually annihilated. We are receiving reports from other civilizations under attack. A massive armada of hostile warships was last spotted heading toward the Andromeda Galaxy. Their destination is unknown, however, their intentions are clear. These forces are extremely dangerous.

"This notification is being sent to members of benevolent civilizations in the inter-galactic community. Beware and stay alert. However, do not get involved. I repeat. Do not get involved. We will send updates to you as we learn more. Any actions we take to defend against hostile incursions will remain secret for security purposes and for the safety of all. These hostile atrocities have forced us to declare war.

"Our intention is to preserve and protect all life and eliminate all threats to our proclaimed purpose of peaceful coexistence. We implore you to stand fast in your convictions and continue focusing on your own individual missions.

"Have faith in our ability to ward off hostile takeovers. We are mobilizing members of the galactic community in the war effort. We Will prevail, punish the perpetrators, and eradicate this evil scourge from our universe.

"We WILL overcome and maintain universal peace under all circumstances. Any suspicious activity that you may encounter should be reported to us immediately. Remain vigilant, alert, and stay safe. Updates and guidance will be forthcoming as deemed necessary.

"Uneek! This message is being sent to you in its totality. Not all member civilizations are receiving the entire message. You were chosen among others to receive the full communication due to your special nature, your essential mission, your proximity to the presence of hostile forces, and your need to know."

Uneek was shocked for several moments upon hearing this news. He was stunned. He pondered about his own purpose and place in the universe. He would continue on his mission as instructed by the CCL. He would not attempt to become a vigilante or a solitary hero in a war of the worlds. He knew he could make a tremendous contribution to the war effort. He had the power and fortitude to do so, but he would refrain. He decided to follow the Celestial Council of Life's orders and guidance. He would not interfere with their agenda. He had confidence in the fact that all intergalactic forces were being mobilized to battle against the hostiles. The war was not his personal or professional mission.

The Luciens had been a wonderful, good-natured civilization, living in peace for millions of years. However, they had made a fatal mistake. They had eliminated all weaponry from their society and planetary governments. Completely defenseless and vulnerable, the Luciens had fallen to a hostile invasion.

Uneek realized that peace could lead to complacency and a false sense of security when no threats are apparent and practically nonexistent for such a long time. They had let their guard down and allowed their unrealistic idealism to take over their common sense. One never knows from where or when a threat will show its ugly face. The universe is vast and full of diverse beings and cultures of all kinds, both good and evil. Uneek had learned not to live in an isolated world of euphoric fantasies and naivety. He maintained a healthy regard for reality. The hostiles found out that the worlds of the Luciens were disarmed, making them easy prey. He knew that defense was vital to self preservation, and that offense is only required when self preservation is threatened. This is the most fundamental tenet of achieving and maintaining peace.

Uneek refocused on his current situation. He had shared the message from the Seven Sisters with Thunder, but the CCL alert notification would remain a secret. He didn't want to ruffle Thunder's feathers any more than was absolutely necessary.

CHAPTER 31

BARB

Awakening early after a refreshing night's sleep, Thunder set out to explore the surrounding woodlands. He was searching for food and water, stopping occasionally along the way to grab mouthfuls of heavily laden, leafy branches of white oak, ash, sugar maple, pine, and fern trees. Berries were particularly pleasing to his voracious palette. Finding quite an expansive strawberry patch, he pulled the entire bush out of the ground, and devoured it whole, including the roots and all. Uneek floated quietly behind Thunder letting him choose the way.

Slowly lumbering forward, Thunder forced his enormous body through large thickets of brush and brambles. He tried to be extra careful as he squeezed between towering trees. However, most were bent over to their limits, some fracturing and crashing down. Others were just accidentally knocked over to make way. Being the behemoth that he was, he left a wide swath of devastation behind him everywhere he went.

After trudging for several miles, Thunder eventually found what he deemed to be the perfect spot. A mass of thick forest with the kind of vegetation most appetizing to him and with a vital source of freshwater, a cool, bubbling stream! He lifted himself up on his haunches, using his tail as an anchor like a tripod, and carefully balancing himself, he slowly hoisted his 15-ton body up until he reached the forest canopy. He snorted and purred with elation as he perused the smorgasbord before him.

Uneek perched against the hefty trunk of a nearby oak tree and savored the warmth of the midday sun. He watched Thunder feed on the abundant foliage and mused to himself. Uneek was happy to see Thunder healing and growing strong again. It was now 3 months since they had reached this part of the country. The long journey from the east coast had been close to impossible for him to accomplish, and the toll it had taken on his body was excruciating. Hopefully, they would be able to continue the last leg of their trek west once Thunder was fully recovered.

Uneek looked up at the trees and playfully asked, "How are you doing, Thunder? Enjoying yourself? It's such a beautiful day!"

Thunder grunted as he greedily masticated a huge mouthful of white ash leaves. After swallowing, he reluctantly replied, "What do you think? Do I look bored or something? Now leave me alone and let me eat! I'm famished, and I'm busy!"

Suddenly, Uneek's attention was drawn away from a lackadaisical daydream by noisy, splashing sounds coming from the center of the bubbling stream. Peering over quizzically at the source of the sound, he was surprised to see a big fish timidly sticking its head out of the water, eyeballing him suspiciously in return. It was treading water incessantly to remain afloat as it studied Uneek.

"Hey! You over there. I'm Barb. Who are you? WHAT are you?"

She continued before Uneek had a chance to respond, "I happen to be the oldest living ray-finned catfish in these here parts." She paused to examine Uneek more closely.

Uneek introduced himself and explained that he was a star. He asked, "Are you called Barb because of your whiskers, 'er I mean barbels?"

Barb loudly retorted, "Don't even go there! I would cut them all off if I didn't need them to survive. I'd be 'clean-shaven' if I had my way! They just happen to serve a vital role in navigation and hunting. Without them I would knock myself out on rocks or who knows what and probably starve to death!"

Unseen and only 30 yards away, Thunder listened patiently to Barb babbling. She DID look like a cat, he realized. In silence and non-verbally, Thunder thought "Meow" in his own mind.

Instantly, Barb blurted out, "No, no! I'm not a cat! Please. I'm a FISH! If I was a cat, what in the world would I be doing swimming in a stream! Cats don't like water. I love my stream! I'm Barb, short for Barbel. Just don't call me Polliwog or Chucklehead!"

"So, you're the oldest 'FISH' around? Just how old does that make you?" Uneek asked.

Barb replied, "I don't really know. I just say that, because all my relatives and friends are deceased. Most were caught, fried, and eaten.

"As I was bottom feeding, minding my own business, I heard voices. And there you were! Do you usually talk to yourself, because I sure don't see anyone else around here? I do a lot of that anymore. I mean, talk to myself. Rocks never respond. I just peeked up out of the water to see what was going on and to check things out. You don't look like anything I have ever seen before in my entire lifetime. Well, maybe up in the sky at night sometimes, but certainly not here. I noticed you weren't holding a long stick with a line hanging over the water either, which is a good thing in my opinion. That's how they all ended up in the frying pan. They were snagged right out of the stream by those nasty hooks, camouflaged with squirming worms and other tasty goodies. I guess you could say, 'they took the bait' and ended up paying dearly for it. After watching you for a while staying submerged, I realized things looked pretty safe, so I popped up and introduced myself."

Uneek surmised that Barb could not see or hear Thunder. But strangely, she had somehow tuned into Thunder's thought of "Meow". A message had telepathically entered Barb's mind, not realizing from where it had come. Uneek had also received the telepathic message as was usual for him.

"My species goes way back. I mean way, way back. Like back to the Late Cretaceous Period, 65 million years ago when my ancestors survived the great extinction."

That's when Thunder involuntarily let the huge, leafy branch he was eating slide out of his mouth, his jaw dropping at the mention of the great extinction. The branch fell crashing loudly to the forest floor causing a moment of unexpected loud commotion. Thunder froze.

Startled, Barb quickly jerked her head around and looked uneasily at the huge branch which had just fallen from a nearby tree for no apparent reason. She scrutinized the tree up and down and then the surrounding area. She was searching for anything that could explain the mysterious incident, barbels twitching uncontrollably. Finally, she just shook her head from side to side. She muttered to herself, "I smell something fishy around here, and it ain't me! I mean really rank! I smell a rat! Some strange, hokey pokey stuff going on around here. I can feel it in my bones!"

Thunder had cautiously dropped his forelegs to the ground. He swung his massive neck around to look at Barb who showed absolutely no sign of noticing him. He sighed, realizing he was invisible to her. Barb's mention of the Late Cretaceous Period had startled him. He had instantly remembered that time like it was yesterday, and Barb had inadvertently gained his full attention.

Barb went on, "Legend proclaims that there was a great extinction caused by a gigantic asteroid impact. It was so powerful that it vibrated the entire planet. It produced a global ash cloud which resulted in an impact winter, years of darkness which led to the utter extinction of 75% of all plant and animal life.

An enormous ash cloud had surrounded the planet blocking sunlight needed for plant and plankton photosynthesis. Flora could no longer make food and died. Most animals starved to death, also becoming extinct. Earth's entire ecosystem and food chain had been disrupted.

Thunder was once again stricken with fear and pain, as his heart pounded in his chest.

"That was a terrible, sad time for all life," Barb continued. "So much misery, death, and suffering. I always cried whenever the elders spoke of it. My species descended from the few survivors of those horrific times."

Thunder was wholly immersed in Barb's story, and he felt deep pangs of sorrow and heartbreak as she recalled the legends and stories handed down to her. At the same time, he felt deeply comforted by her telling the story. Up to this time, he had only recollected his own experience; he had never 'heard' the story told by anyone else. Yes, it was comforting in a strange way.

She paused for a long moment deep in thought, and then defiantly concluded, "At least it got rid of all those huge monsters that roamed and terrorized the earth! Cold-blooded murderous beasts!"

At this sudden reproach of his ancestors, Thunder burst out in tears. He sobbed to himself, "Yes, we were the magnificent, glorious rulers of Earth for 200 million years! We dominated the entire Mesozoic Era from 252 million years ago until 66 million years ago! It was the Age of Dinosaurs! The Age of Conifers! And then we were no more. I am no more."

"To change the subject, do you care for fish?" Barb asked Uneek.

"Yes, I love fish," replied Uneek.

Barb's eyes grew as big as saucers, and she backed up trembling in fear.

Noticing her distress, Uneek quickly added, "I care for fish, but I don't eat them. In fact, I don't eat anything, period."

With a big sigh of relief, Barb exclaimed, "I've been so fortunate today. Luck is on my side! Holy polliwog! I guess I'll live to see another day after all!"

Abruptly and without any warning, Barb dipped back under the water and swam briskly away, but not before yelling behind her, "You are WEIRD Uneek! WEIRD lookin', and WEIRD actin'! You are hokey! See you later, WEIRDO! I'm outta here!"

Uneek and Thunder looked at each other in astonishment. Wiping away his tears and snorting out the phlegm from his runny nose, Thunder eyed Uneek. They both burst out hysterically laughing, tears of joy now replacing Thunder's tears of sorrow. Uneek was thankful inwardly that Barb was gone. Thunder didn't need anymore reminders of his painful past. Chuckling, Uneek said to Thunder, "If she only knew there was one of those 'cold-blooded murderous monsters standing within 30 yards of her! Can you imagine if she saw the size of the 'rat' she smelled?"

They slowly headed back to camp in silence, their minds teeming with thoughts and questions about the encounter with Barb. As they retired beside the fire, Thunder said to Uneek, "So thoughts can actually travel not only through time and space, but also through dimensions? Mind can traverse the universe?"

This was an epiphany for Thunder, and Uneek just replied, "Yes, they can."

Uneek knew that ESP was diverse and limitless. It was perception beyond the physical realm. Every lifeform in the universe possessed extrasensory systems, and each was unique.

What Thunder had just experienced with Barb was a sudden revelation to

him. Deep in thought, he was content and as quiet as a mouse. The night brought silence. He had finally exhausted his endless rambling for today. His mind was empty with no interference. The images of the past were loosening their grip on him. His encounter with Barb confirmed his ability to communicate outside of the dimension in which he was imprisoned. His mind was becoming fluid again; the mind freeze was thawing. Uneek had come to Earth and was saving him.

The locked door to the universe and salvation was finally opening up for him! He had always had faith, but now he also had hope.

Uneek glanced inconspicuously over at Thunder and sighed. He was fast asleep. Looking up at the stars, Uneek wondered when he would get a reply from his home nebula and thought, "Life in the universe is an enigma."

CHAPTER 32
THUNDER'S REQUEST

Uneek and Thunder eventually left the meadow to search for a place to hunker down for the night. Following the stream, they found a spot within a couple of miles from where they had met Barb. Thunder's face instantly lit up when he noticed the bounty of succulent vegetation, bearing sweet, fragrant fruit.

Uneek set up camp, while Thunder drank his fill from the little stream's crystal, clear water. Moonlight flickered and danced playfully off of the stream's gently rippling flow. Thunder ingested several mouthfuls of rocks and pebbles from the stream's bed and banks, before he settled down to eat. He pulled off leafy, peach laden branches from a nearby tree, swallowing them whole. He had no teeth to actually chew. The stones in his stomach would aid in digestion. After eating several full, leafy bushes, he lifted himself up on his enormous haunches to peruse the treetops. In the meantime, Uneek had gathered a pile of dry twigs, sticks, and branches, breaking them down to small pieces. He started to build a fire, lighting the small, carefully stacked pile by touching it with a small burst of concentrated energy. The kindling slowly grew into a nice sized blaze.

Thunder's hunger pains subsided, and He made his way to the enticing warmth of the campfire. Darkness was slowly creeping in, and the night air was becoming chilly. Thunder was a reptile, an ectothermic herbivore, whose body temperature was directly dependent on the temperature of the surrounding environment. His body could not generate its own heat like endotherms. He was cold-blooded and his body temperature was dropping. He moved into close proximity to the fire to warm up. The sun had set.

Uneek watched as Thunder struggled to find the perfect, most comfortable distance to the fire, moving his massive body around the flames several times before he finally laid down. Unlike endotherms, whose body temperature was regulated by internal heat generation, Thunder had to regulate his own body temperature, using his innate sense of thermoregulation.

Both having settled in, Uneek reduced his energy output and slowly dimmed.

They talked long into the night, telling stories of paranormal events that each had experienced throughout their lifetimes.

Eventually Thunder asked, "Would it be okay if I shared my deepest thoughts with you, maybe tomorrow or the following night? I just feel like I have to get it all off my chest, out of my mind and stop letting it eat at me. I'm just too tired tonight to even start."

Uneek replied, "Sure. I'll be ready when you are. Just say when. I'll listen to anything and everything you have to say. We all need an outlet sometimes. I don't mind being your sounding board. I'm here for you, buddy, whenever you are up to it."

Thunder was relieved to hear Uneek's willingness and sighed deeply, exhaling a blast of hot air. He replied, "Maybe soon."

CHAPTER 33
THE PARANORMAL

The next day Thunder continued his train of thought, picking up where he had left off the night before. He immediately jumped in to dominate the conversation that Uneek was trying to have on a completely different topic.

"Just because something can't be proven, does not necessarily mean that it does not exist or is not true or real. Denial is prevalent in the scientific community, as well as in religion, and even in social life. Many don't believe in things that they can't see for themselves, and they discount them as 'hogwash'. They demand to be shown proof. Many truths are subsequently swept under the rug. Ridicule often ensues when the truth falls too far outside of their limited realm of comprehension."

Thunder went on to say, "What I experience is what I know to be real and true. I may not necessarily understand what I've experienced, but I know I did."

"For example, I've seen spaceships from other worlds for as long as I can remember. Maybe when we're star gazing out West in Big Sky Country, I'll tell you about some of these encounters. Many experiences are 'unique' to certain 'unique' individuals!" They both laughed at the pun.

Thunder eventually continued, "Some things are esoteric and sacred, not realized even during an entire lifetime. Some things that happen cannot be explained in words. They can only be experienced, felt, and realized. We know very little, when it comes right down to it. What we don't know is so much greater than what we do know. What we know is like one, small grain of sand on an endless beach. I get so infuriated, when I watch humans walking around with their inflated egos, acting like idiots. Nothing but pea heads! Little heads with big egos! They don't have a clue!" They both erupted again in a burst of roaring laughter, having visuals of humans with little peas for heads.

"All things are unknown until they are known. Humans are afraid of the unknown. Experience is the best teacher. The fear of the unknown is the greatest hindrance to learning. I'm talking about the universe! It is the huge unknown. Humans have barely taken their first steps into the 'eerie' vastness of space. I've never given much credibility to the intellectual ramblings of egotistical human beings. They think they know everything. They revel in the accolades of their academic achievements and so-called 'expertise'. Just book learners with their itsy-bitsy grasp of reality. Many never venture out from behind their books. They remain hidden deep within their little protective boxes, their pods. They live life in books, kind of like people do who watch soap operas all day long, never venturing out into the teal world to pursue their dreams. They never learn how to harness the natural potential of their own minds. They want everything handed to them on silver platters, without expending the time and energy required to explore the world for themselves. The development of talent and the mind takes time, perseverance, and unwavering dedication. There is no such thing as a born artist, born genius, or born scientist. It's hard work, and it cannot just be handed over. Most remain with their noses stuck in their books or in front of the TV, watching others live their lives. It's like a father wanting his son to be a star quarterback, regardless of what the child dreams of or wants. They refuse to believe anything that doesn't fit into their little worlds. Pea heads!

"And then to make it worse, they hold what little they do know over each others' heads with attitudes of superiority. They may have college degrees, make lots of money or be popular, but what they have actually learned is not much, when it comes to the big picture. Some of this is the result of a system that stove pipes education. They put all of their energy into learning only one skill, one trade, or one ability, so they can "fit" into a manmade system and find their niche in society. In this way, they can make money to secure their survival in this world. Most view their professions as their lives. It's just a job!"

Uneek had fallen fast asleep again, bored to death with Thunder's ranting and raving. Most of the human aspects that Thunder was incessantly complaining about were not limited to the human race. They existed in almost every civilization in the universe. Uneek knew this but did not have the heart to tell Thunder. To Thunder, it was his own special perspective, and he knew he was right. He needed to get it all out of his system. Talking and sharing his feelings with someone gave Thunder a sense of confidence and pride in himself. His convictions needed to be voiced. His deflated self worth and self esteem were nourished in this way. He needed a good listener, someone to share his innermost thoughts and opinions with.

Thunder didn't even notice that Uneek had fallen asleep, and he continued, totally enthralled with this subject, enjoyably venting. He was on a roll in an oblivious, elated stupor. The chance to express himself was absolutely euphoric! And to have someone to actually talk to who listened and understood was the best thing that had happened to him in the past millions of years!

Uneek lay fast asleep, also in an oblivious stupor, but he was dreaming of something completely different and heavenly.

CHAPTER 34
SCIENCE VERSUS RELIGION

Sometime during the following evening, as Thunder and Uneek were lounging by the fire, the topic of scientific method and empirical evidence came up again. These were both aspects of human thought processes that were designed to provide proof of the existence of whatever was being studied and/or questioned.

After much discussion, they both agreed that not all things could be scientifically proven with the limited palette of knowledge and resources that humans currently had to work with.

Thunder said, "As of yet, they don't even have the ability to prove, disapprove or accurately measure the existence of spiritual or paranormal phenomena. This is because these aspects of reality are not manifested or grounded in matter. You can't grab heaven in your fist!

"Humans flit about haphazardly like flies around a light bulb trying to figure it out! They see something there that shines and sparks their curiosity, but they don't understand what it is. Humans have spent thousands of years walking around in circles, trying to figure it all out. It's when you don't know, that you really know, and when you think you know, you don't. It's a complete conundrum, a paradox!

"Besides, attempts to hypothesize the nature of the macrocosm or the microcosm, eventually always end up in a whirlwind of probabilities. Inevitably, the result is pure speculation and conjecture. Theories about the spiritual world as well as the natural world abound, but none can be proven, supported or confirmed by contemporary empirical testing. That is because everything is in constant flux, forever changing. Nothing ever remains the same, always transforming. They can't get their grasp on it. They need to just go with the flow. Humans are not the owners of the universe. Not the greatest creation. Only a small part of an inconceivable eternity."

Thunder thought to himself, as Uneek dosed off for a while. Thunder reflected on the controversy between advocates of scientific methodology and those of spirituality. They oppose each other in their absoluteness of principles. They lie at the opposite ends of the spectrum and have been at odds with each other for thousands of years. In the past, science and religion were of one and the same reality, knowledge totally interwoven. A rift came when science and religion parted ways over the nature of reality - one adamantly adhering to an omnipotent and omniscient God or gods and the other searching for the God particle! The macro versus the micro, all in the same.

Uneek roused and spontaneously recited a poem:

"Powder puffs a cloud into hills and plains,
As tender touches on the flute in springtime ease explains;
The whisper of life in ripening slow,
decays the fruit for further flame,
And the changing seasons with miracles held,
bring forth new life in all the same."

"Wow!" Thunder's ears were perked up. "That was beautiful! Where did you hear that poem?"

"Just made it up right now in my mind," replied Uneek.

"It says it all in a nutshell! I wish I could create and recite poetry ss easily as you."

Uneek assured him, "You can, but you don't know you can. You speak poetry all the time, Thunder, when you ramble. Poetry doesn't have to rhyme. It flows as easily as time does."

Thunder reflected on that statement for a while. Then he said, "Human thought is further subdivided into separate schools of thought, each purporting to be the way to truth. In fact, they are all just a small piece of the puzzle, the truth of the whole pie. The cosmos envelops all these schools of thought under its massive umbrella. Just like you said, 'in all the same.' They are all interconnected in the fabric of reality, the nature of which is yet unfathomable to humans.

"Humans have been taught to think deductively, breaking everything down into its individual parts. However, there are innumerable ways of thinking. A totally opposite way of thinking is inductive thinking. It puts all the pieces together which combines parts into a more expansive, inclusive reality. There we go again. The micro versus the macro, linear thinking in one direction or the other. What about all the other dimensions beyond 3D?"

Thunder looked at Uneek and asked, "Is the stuff we are made of eternal? Wouldn't that possibility bring the scientists and the theologians back together again? Like the analogy of religious belief in life everlasting in comparison to the belief in an eternal cosmos?"

Uneek looked over and grinned at Thunder saying, "Yes, in all the same."

CHAPTER 35

SAY WHEN

Thunder flatly said to Uneek, "When." He waited for a response.

"When what?" Uneek asked.

Thunder had been mumbling to himself all day long, stomping his heavy feet on the ground with every step. He couldn't contain his thoughts any longer.

"When is now! You told me to say 'when' before I started telling you my thoughts about humans. You said you would listen," Thunder blurted out.

"Oh. That's what you mean. Yes, I did, and I'm ready," Uneek replied.

Thunder immediately launched into a tirade of emotions, pent up anger, and disgust. He poured out his thoughts like an endless, running faucet. Uneek was more than willing to listen, as he had promised he would.

Thunder babbled on and on about humans and their manmade systems.

"Once 'retired', if fortunate enough to reach that pinnacle in life, humans don't know what to do with themselves. They expend all their energy in pursuit of money, promotions, and advancement in the system, preparing for their chance at the glory days. No more work! And what for? More money. A person only needs so much money to live. It all boils down to how you want to live and how much you want to give. The glory days are always here. They never went anywhere.

"Many feel empty, lonely, and lost. They never develop their own talents, the creative gifts they were born with. They just work for the man their whole lives, giving up all their talents and energy in exchange for money. Humans are spiritual, mental vampires, sucking the energy out of everyone around them like black holes. Instead of shining like stars, they fill the endless void of darkness within themselves with the energy they siphon off of others. Give me your soul, and I'll give you a couple of bucks!

"Those at the very top of the manmade systems, control the world economically. They secure their finances by means of control. They use threats of demotion, termination, and sometimes even death to maintain their wealth. I've seen it happen a million times. The financial grip they have on humanity is a staggering realization to behold!

"The financial empire has its mitts in every aspect of human existence. Food, shelter, clothing, energy, water, healthcare, and medicine. You name it, they control it. Even their minds and spirits are squeezed in the clamps of the vice. The system steals their minds, their creativity, their natural spirituality and freedom. All these human resources are used to advance their own place in the financial empire. To be employed means to allow oneself to be used. Everyone wants to be rich! But the price of the pursuit is destroying the unity of humanity and the world! Humans are pitted against each other in a competitive system of personal gain. Bees and ants put humans to shame. They work together harmoniously in pursuit of a common goal, the survival of their species.

"They put taboos on certain thoughts and beliefs that challenge their control. This happens in established religion and education, in the military, and business world. Humans are called out as undesirables, when they challenge the fairness of the controlling processes involved. Being disgruntled is not good. To be a whistleblower is the worst. Heyla, the unions and the media!

"Most humans are unknowingly brainwashed by established education, religion, and business. The powers that be use threats, ridicule, and peer pressure to maintain acceptable social standards of behavior. Many have lost their own minds to these abject forces of total indoctrination and control.

"Humans need to be more careful with their most precious asset, their minds! They need to protect their individuality, their uniqueness. They need to look inside themselves to find their own truth, not adopt the truths of others. Humans should lead themselves and follow their own calling.

"They should be searching for the true reality which exists everywhere, outside of the manmade system. It lies in nature. What they are being taught is not the truth! They need to search for and find their own voices and reconnect to their true selves, not lose their minds to these evil forces of greed and control. They lose themselves as they grow up.

"History is written by the victors. The truth is actually found in the recesses of human suffering, in the stories and tales of the victims, the unjustly oppressed and persecuted!

"I hate when people ask children, 'What are you going to be when you grow up?' It offends my intelligence. It offends me. In other words, 'What are you going to do to fit into the system and make money?' Children are already what they are meant to be. They are gifted human beings. Their individual energy should be developed and nurtured, not used and altered to fit in somewhere in manmade systems. They should grow according to their own talents, in their own way and in their own time. They need to bloom into beautiful, unique individuals. Well, here's a list of things you can become. Pick one and go for it. But make sure you pick one that makes a lot of money! They were born, and because of this, they already fit in and are someone!"

Thunder rambled on, "Money is not produced by nature. It is a human invention and not natural. It is used to control nature humans. The financial empire charges humans for practically everything they need to survive. But not the air yet, unless they are on ventilators or use oxygen tanks. If pollution of the air is not reversed, clean air will become the newest commodity that will be sold to humans.

"Programmed humans are the most valuable assets in this system. Subservient, obedient 'yes' people. These types of humans are essential to propagate the growth and maintain the processes and structures of control. Little do they know, though. Ultimately, they are NOT in control at all, and deep down, they are starting to realize it. They are just biding their time, trying to make as much money as possible, before the world changes or ends. They are aware that other, more intelligent, technologically and spiritually advanced beings exist in the universe and are here on Earth. The ETs are making contact with thousands of humans every day. The benevolent ones are providing guidance and help to Earthlings. There is no sanctity in the financial empire, when it is corrupt. There is no sanctity in weapon systems that kill innocent life. There is no sanctity in destroying nature. These beings have been preparing humans for advancement into the cosmos, the real world. I've seen them several times! They do exist! The brainwashing and denial cannot stand much longer when these beings can appear at will to whomever and whenever they choose. Those in power have no control over when or where this occurs.

"They have been aiding humans in their development, technologically and spiritually for thousands of years. They know that the human race and the planet are in danger. The knowledge of ET presence here on Earth is escalating."

Thunder stopped at that instant, realizing he had lost his audience. He had been talking to himself. He didn't know for how long. He looked over at Uneek, who had completely dimmed out. He had so much more to share with Uneek. Things that he had observed and learned about the humans that he felt were vital. All he wanted to share would have to wait for now. They were topics for another day.

He stretched his neck over and grabbed a mouthful of dried sticks and a couple of logs from Uneek's woodpile, dropping them carefully onto the smoldering fire. His eyelids got heavy as the fire slowly started up again. He lay back and turned off the faucet, his mind feeling somewhat freer and less clogged. He fell into a deep sleep with visions of spaceships flying through the stars and galaxies. He wasn't cognizant that his new friend, Uneek, the one he had lately been sharing his soul with, was a benevolent ET himself.

CHAPTER 36
THE GOOD STUFF

Uneek had decided to spend a few more weeks in camp, before they headed out again. Thunder had to relax and continue regaining his strength, physically, mentally, and spiritually. Uneek figured this was the best place for him to be able to do that.

Thunder seemed to be enjoying this reprieve, spending all day eating, drinking, and slumbering, and unfortunately, spending all night talking. Not a word, though, had been spoken about the journey that lay ahead. Not a peep from Thunder, just a little small talk in between naps and snacks. His light seemed to come on at night, when he started up again with his long, delirious raves. Many times in the last couple of weeks, he couldn't stop talking, pulling all-nighters and sleeping all day. Uneek thought to himself, "Was Thunder purposely avoiding the subject of travel?"

They were relaxing next to the stream by camp, when Thunder said, "You fell asleep on me again the other night, right when I was getting into the good stuff."

Uneek said defensively, "You were rambling on and on, and the droning sound of your voice put me out like a light. It was definitely not a two-way conversation, and I was getting tired. Sorry."

Uneek knew that Thunder hadn't been able to speak to anyone for eons and was bursting at the seams. He would just let him speak his mind and listen, totally bored and already knowing most everything he was hearing. Thunder needed to let it all out. No matter how long it took, Uneek would stand by him and try to listen. Uneek sat down propping his back up against a tree. He looked at Thunder and said, "Okay. I'm ready. "

Thunder said, "Let me continue explaining myself from where I left off the other night."

Uneek replied, "How can you possibly remember where you left off? That was two days ago!"

"Well, I know you don't have a clue where I left off, because you were zonked out! But trust me. I remember exactly where I left off, when I realized you were asleep, unconscious to the world and to me.

"I was talking about true knowledge. It cannot be found in an atom, or in mathematical equations, or up each others' asses.

"Sorry for putting it that way, but it's true! Humans have the tendency to park themselves up each others' butts, hiding from the world like ostriches sticking their heads into holes in the ground. They feel content, safe, and comfortable there, hiding from everyone and everything. There is so much to be discovered, with all life's trials and tribulations. AND all the amazing gifts to be found, talents to be developed. Struggle builds character. So much work to be done to clean up his mess.

"Humans like this are weak in character and spirit, falling apart at the drop of a pin. Humans need to grow and become strong individuals, not hide behind or within others.

"Love and friendship exhibit the most beautiful human states of being that exist. These special, human relationships need to be nurtured, and care should be taken not to allow them to fall into dysfunctional dependency. Maintaining healthy relationships requires attention to individual freedom, allowing each other to pursue their own dreams independently as well as together. People need to learn and grow at their own pace. It requires supporting one another in reaching their own full potential, to achieve self-actualization. Each is born alone, and each will die alone. But during their lifetimes, they cling to each other for dear life, smothering the spark of life in the process. They die, their destinies unfulfilled, only to have to come back and try again.

The mood around camp had become somber as Thunder's wisdom poured forth. Uneek listened intently absorbing it all and pondering these aspects of human life and behavior. Uneek was learning. He had always been an individual, standing on his

own. He found many human habits to be absurd and counter productive. This line of Thunder's talk was exactly what he had wanted to hear. It was extremely interesting and informative. He didn't understand these human tendencies. To him, humans wasted precious time and spiritual energy in just "having fun". They seemed to be destructive behaviors that lead to absolutely no benefit to humanity's problems or spiritual progression in the cosmos. There was so much work to be done, so much that needed to be achieved.

The act of procreation was designed solely to have offspring, not to be a lustful addiction, mindlessly consumed by the dictates of their hormones. It had become the main focus of many. The glue that held some people together in this way was selfish, and it separated them from the rest of humanity and the world. Humans had to get their 'fix', just like a drug addict or an alcoholic. These addictions were the cause of humanity's inability to transcend to higher levels of being, not only as individuals, but as a civilization.

Uneek reflected on the common housefly. It laid its eggs in decaying carcasses, providing the perfect birthplace to sustain the lives of the maggots that hatched. To him, this analogy also demonstrated the human condition. Overpopulation on a dying planet with no accountability for widescale hunger, suffering, and unwanted children conveniently disposed of. He had never come across an advanced civilization that kills their own unborn. Humans were supposed to be more advanced, yet they were irresponsible and despicable when it came to their reproductive systems. They sought only to satisfy their own individual desires. Uncontrolled, selfish moments of pleasure were happening constantly all over the planet with no regard for the possible consequences. The act of procreation had become an acceptable habit of human interaction. Humans were inept and weak in spirit, constantly medicating themselves with sex, drugs, alcohol, and money. Thunder had previously shared all this information with Uneek, and the reality of the human condition was abhorrent to him. Instead of using their brains, they were controlled and consumed by their own hormonal highs and addictions.

"Humans needed to learn to disengage their minds from their bodies and to avoid the pitfalls of the flesh. Spiritual strength comes from manifesting mind over matter. They needed to pursue higher levels of spiritual and mental growth. In the end, disengagement from their bodies would happen to them anyway and naturally when they died.

"The popular saying 'I'm only human' is a ridiculous, superfluous excuse for weak humans to shirk responsibility to grow and evolve. It serves to enable their subhuman, miserable existence. They use this excuse to support all their misgivings, failures, and undesirable actions. They have no clue of their own human capabilities, the inherent gifts that were bestowed on them when they were created, nor their ultimate destiny.

"They don't want to change. They would rather stagnate, remaining the same in an endless cycle of addictive, dysfunctional behaviors. Uneek had learned about these things during previous, long talks with Thunder, whose knowledge of human behavior was profound. Maybe this was the cause of the lack of spiritual growth in humans, leading to their inability to advance in the spiritual realm. Many of the inhabitants of Earth were hostile and violence abounded, mot only amongst each other, but also in every aspect of human life. It was uncommon for a species to be so heartless and hostile to each other, let alone the world around them. Thunder had shared some of the insights of William Shakespeare with him. He wrote that the act of sex is an expense of the spirit. William also had warned to 'love moderately' in his tragedy, 'Romeo and Juliet'.

It seemed that Shakespeare possessed some of the same opinions that Thunder was expressing."

When Uneek turned his attention back to Thunder, he was still talking, unaware of Uneek's temporary mental absence, as he took time to process all of this information.

Uneek tuned back in as Thunder stated, "Reality is right in front of them, staring them in the face! And they just don't see it or want to see it. They would rather languish in their comfort zones as others and the test of the world suffers. Denial, apathy, and selfishness are the means of maintaining their way of life.

"There's never been any real gain without struggle. You know they say no one changes unless the pain of remaining the same is greater than the pain incurred by changing. They're just growing pains, my friend! Growing pains of giving up habits and comfort zones on the way to pursuing greater, better states of being, so to say. This is what I was talking about!"

CHAPTER 37
THE INDIGENOUS CONNECTION

Eagle Eye removed the arrows from the two rabbits he had killed and stuffed them into his quiver. He secured the rabbits under his loin cloth belt. He would return later with several friends to haul the dead deer back to the village.

As was the custom of native people, every part of the animals they killed would be used to ensure survival.

Indigenous people had the highest regard and respect for life and the animals they killed. With a deep sense of reverence, they only killed what was absolutely necessary to survive, never for sport. Native people were staunch believers in the practice of "no waste, no want." This belief system not only supported their own lives, but also the continued survival of the animals.

Eagle Eye continued to scout the perimeter of the forest, when he noticed a huge shadow where there should be none. He knew the woods well and was confused as the shadow moved about. He proceeded cautiously, perusing his surroundings for the source of the shadow. Involuntarily, he suddenly jumped backward in surprise and instant fear! In front of him was a gigantic beast standing in the nearby clearing. The beast's chest rose high overhead, and it was propped upright on its rear haunches. It's neck and head extended even further upward into the canopy of white oak trees. Eagle Eye cowered in sheer terror! Breathless and motionless, he stared upward in disbelief, internally battling with the reality of what he was seeing.

The creature dropped down on all fours with a tremendous jolt, vibrating the ground beneath him. This revealed a glowing light, hovering in midair behind the beast! The light resembled a tiny, rising star, as it floated up to the creature and asked, "Are you done yet? Can we please continue and finally be on our way again?"

The beast burst out a loud, powerful snort, unknowingly blowing Eagle Eye off of his feet! The creature reluctantly answered, "Yes, I guess so! How much further? Do you even know where we are going?"

Discreetly picking himself up from the ground and hiding behind a wide, tree trunk, Eagle Eye was unsure what to do. Should he approach and make his presence known, or should he let them pass in silence? The star seemed kind and gentle, but the beast was unruly and angry.

Uneek replied, "No, not really. But we are still traveling right on track, according to the directions that the Seven Sisters gave me."

"If you ask me, we're lost, Uneek! This is ridiculous! I need a vacation! You know what? I'm just going to stay here. You go on ahead, and when and IF you ever find the village, come back and get me. In the meanwhile, I'll be here eating and relaxing."

At the mention of the Pleiadians, Eagle Eye yelled out at Uneek, "Wait!"

Uneek and Thunder were led to a native village by the astute youth. Surprisingly, both Uneek and Thunder were visible and audible to him and his tribe.

The young brave had introduced himself as Eagle Eye, his village's most gifted hunter and scout. After listening to a shortened version of their long quest and realizing their special nature, Eagle Eye wished to help them.

The way to Eagle Eye's village was not far, but Thunder lagged behind, continuously complaining and having to find alternate routes around densely wooded areas. Once reunited in a meadow about a mile from the village, the three finally arrived at the outskirts of the settlement together. The tribesmen, women, and children stared in horror, as the behemoth emerged from a bend and approached. It was immediately regarded as an ominous sign, and they quickly ran off, screaming in terror.

Uneek's brilliance, and their reaction to Thunder's gigantic size made them the most peculiar sight the tribe had ever seen. They followed Eagle Eye into the heart of the village, despite the extremely guarded reception. Looking intimidated and wearily suspicious, they all kept a safe distance from Thunder, who found their fear amusing. He snorted at them several times, chuckling as he watched them flee, shrieking with contorted faces.

Eagle Eye told Uneek and Thunder to stay put, as he made his way to a large wattle and daub building in the center of the village. He pulled open the door and solemnly stepped inside. After a short while, he reappeared and signaled for Uneek and Thunder to come forward. An elderly, distinguished man, adorned with a splendid headdress of colorful feathers and beads, eventually stepped out. He was accompanied by several tribesmen, who walked cautiously beside and behind him. Despite Thunder's incredible size and Uneek's strange countenance, the group of tribesmen nodded as Eagle Eye said, "Our tribe welcomes you both. May I introduce our tribal Chief and Wise One, Bright Wolf."

Uneek and Thunder nodded back with reverence and gratitude, as Bright Wolf greeted them saying, "Welcome to our village. It has been many moons since I've seen your kind," he said looking directly at Uneek. Peering up at Thunder, he said, "And I've never actually seen your kind alive before, only painted on rock and cave wall drawings by our ancestors. This is certainly an extraordinary occasion. Eagle Eye has briefly informed me of your journey and quest. We will speak more about your intentions. Come."

It was an honor to be permitted council with the village Wise One. The distant crowd of timid spectators slowly calmed down, as Uneek and Thunder followed Bright Wolf closer to his tribe's meeting place. Bright Wolf felt honored in turn and beamed with pride and amazement. He thought to himself, "A star being and a live prehistoric beast! What unexpected guests! The Great Spirit works in mysterious ways."

Eagle Eye immediately took leave to gather help with the dead deer still laying on the forest floor, lest it started decaying.

Uneek was invited to enter Bright Wolf's meeting house, where they could speak in private. The others remained around the campfire outside, engaged in speculative conversations. Thunder stayed close by, indulging in another feast of white oak leaves, juicy berry bushes, succulent shrubs, and an abundance of conifers.

Once safely seated inside in front of a slow burning fire, Bright Wolf spoke, "It's been a long time since I encountered a star being. Our ancestors, the star people, descended to Earth from the sky thousands of years ago. We remain in close contact with each other to this day. Our connection to the star peoples and the Great Spirit of the universe is sacred."

Scrutinizing Uneek more closely, he asked, "And how are you called?"

"I am Uneek."

The Chief replied, "Yes, as we all are in our own ways."

Uneek said, "Yes. But my name is actually 'Uneek'. That is how I am called."

Bright Wolf raised his eyebrows and said, "You are different from the other sky people I know. Where do you arise from?"

Uneek explained his distant origin, the Esoterica Nebula, and his long journey to Earth.

"The sky people I communicate with are from star systems much, much closer than your nebula. Why have you come to Earth?"

Uneek told the Chief of his mission and also his search for Gaia.

"Ah! Gaia! The Mother of the Universe, Mother Nature! The Great Nurturer Gaia, keeping all the natural forces of creation in balance. She is a close friend of mine and has taught me much about understanding the ways of the universe. How to heal my people of sickness, physical and mental. She taught us about conservation and appreciation for all life. So, you search for her. Why?"

Uneek replied, "Yes. We need her help." He explained Thunder's space time, dimensional disconnect. "The Seven Sisters of the Pleiades led me here to you."

"The Pleiadians! My dear, sacred sisters! I know them well. They are multidimensional, spiritual beings. They have come here many times to visit. They led you to me, because they know I am friends with Gaia and am able to help you, as they told you. This is true."

Suddenly, Bright Wolf began humming the harmonious, Sister's song that Uneek knew so well, and he joined in. Their combined humming became a beautiful tribute to them and the universe. A profound spiritual transcendency occurred, elevating them to higher realms of consciousness. They remained in the state of meditation, ascending to levels of pure spiritual awareness. They became spirit brothers, and their bond became forever forged in truth and light.

Delightfully reveling in spiritual bliss, Bright Wolf slowly reached behind him and brought forth a rolled-up piece of hide. He unrolled the hide and handed it carefully to Uneek saying, "Follow this painted, pictorial map.

"It will guide you to Gaia. She can be found beyond the mountains, as depicted here in the distance. You will come to the Tree of Vines. This is where you will summon Gaia. Keep calling out to her, for she is very busy and could be dwelling anywhere in the eternal universe. She will appear as a beautiful woman garbed in nature's finest bounty. She will come to you and help you and Thunder." Uneek made a permanent imprint of the map in his mind.

Suddenly, Thunder asked loudly from outside of the dwelling, "Is it far from here? I can't take another long journey across the country like the one we just experienced!"

Bright Wolf answered, "Not far. Two, three days journey from here at the most. Except for the hills, the way is open, flat country. The mountains are old and well-rounded. You will have no problem getting there."

Uneek was relieved that Bright Wolf had taken it upon himself to explain and persuade Thunder, who continued his eating spree at the abundant, Tennessee smorgasbord.

Emerging from the long house, Bright Wolf and Uneek joined Thunder. Expressing gratitude for showing him the guide map, farewells and blessings were exchanged. Then, Uneek and Thunder headed toward the forest again to search for a resting spot for the evening.

Following the map in his mind, they came upon the waterfall, where they decided to set up camp for the night.

Thunder immediately waded into the shallow lake, laying down to soak his aching muscles and tired bones. A fire was started, and they settled in, but only after another one of Thunder's lengthy feeding frenzies. He stretched his neck up along each side of the waterfall, where the succulent foliage grew opulently. Before returning to the blazing campfire, he took an enormous drink, allowing the pristine water to fall directly down his throat. He planned to take another leisurely soak in the morning, before they set out again. The day had been long and surprisingly eventful. Exhausted from the day's journey, Thunder settled beside the fire and fell deep asleep in short order. Satisfied with what they had accomplished so far, Uneek lay transfixed on the night sky. He sorted out the overwhelming stream of thoughts bombarding his mind. He had to muster all his faith in order to face the uncertainties in his future. Allowing the subtle, natural rhythm of the planet permeate his soul, he felt a soothing peace come to him. The only sounds were the crackling fire, crickets, and the hypnotizing water splashing down from the falls. No snoring for an unusual change. Uneek was soon carried away to the world of dreams.

CHAPTER 38

GAIA FOUND

They had finally found Gaia, closely adhering to Bright Wolf's instructions and referring to recollections of the pictorial map.

After hours of channeling and summoning her at the Tree of Vines and with almost unbearable anticipation and great patience, Gaia finally appeared in her splendid glory.

She personified herself physically as a female entity of magnificent beauty, the air rippling all around her. Surrounded by a natural aura of light, her presence was electrifying. Her manifestation of powerful, universal forces was displayed as a mirage-like energy field, at times hazy and wavering, as it oscillated between dimensions. In this way, she introduced herself as Mother Nature. "You can call me Gaia. What is so important that you have summoned me?"

Uneek and Thunder were both mesmerized by her natural beauty and unspeakable power. Yet, Gaia's demeanor was gentle.

Thunder stuttered nervously in a lame attempt to introduce himself. Hearing himself, he quickly fell silent, reaching his head high to grab a hanging branch of leaves. That would keep his mouth busy.

Bowing with the deepest of respect, Uneek humbly answered Gaia. Her imploring gaze remained steady as Uneek said, "This is my friend, Thunder, and I am Uneek. We summoned you because we need help. We were referred to you by the Pleiadians and Bright Wolf."

Gaia nodded in approval and smiled. "What exactly is the nature of your problem?"

Uneek explained the space time warp that Thunder was experiencing as best he could.

Gaia spoke, "I apologize for the delay. I was preoccupied with assessing a dangerous situation developing in several areas of the universe." Not another word was uttered by Gaia about it. Glancing quickly at Uneek, she sensed his awareness of the hostile problem. Uneek was uncontrollably enamored by her deep, kaleidoscopic eyes when her gaze locked with his. A subtle stream of energy passed between them. Thunder could feel it, too, but didn't understand exactly what it meant. He snorted softly to himself.

This amiable introduction to each other precipitated a lengthy, in-depth exchange of information. Thunder had joined in, no longer nervous or stuttering.

Gaia began to speak. She presented a brief account of what was happening on Earth due to human ignorance. The realization of what may happen to Earth was deeply troubling to Gaia. She loved and cared for all life on Earth and throughout the universe. To lose a beautiful planet like Earth and all its occupants would be a devastating event, having unforeseen consequences throughout the Sun system and galaxy.

"Planets have been destroyed before, some by warfare, others by natural disasters, and some by the ignorance of their own misguided inhabitants. Interstellar and galactic wars are inevitable in a universe teeming with intelligent and super intelligent lifeforms, sometimes at odds with each other. These wars could lead to complete annihilation of heavenly bodies along with their diversified lifeforms." Gaia peered again at Uneek streaming concern about the recent hostile attacks.

Gaia went on, "The original planet that existed between Mars and Jupiter in the Sun system, was destroyed in such a war, leaving only fragments of what was once a beautiful, vibrant world. It was reduced to an orbiting asteroid belt.

"These destructive wars also had a tremendous and devastating effect on neighboring heavenly bodies. Mars still shows signs of these warring times. Earth shifted on its axis, causing an instant, world-wide cataclysm. Siberian mastodons have been discovered under layers of ice with mouths and stomachs full of vegetation that they had been eating when they were instantly frozen."

Gaia didn't want to see the further destruction of Earth by the human race or by any other off-planet, belligerent beings with their high-tech weapons. Gaia went on to explain that all natural processes and disasters, no matter how big and powerful or how small, eventually settle back into equilibrium and homeostasis.

Uneek reflected on the essence of Gaia as he stared at her. The universe is a miraculous, fail-safe and dynamic system. Gaia constituted the very fabric of energy. Gaia WAS "change", the only constant. The universe and everything in it is "alive".

Uneek and Thunder listened patiently to Gaia's concerns and words of wisdom. Suddenly, she fell silent. Regaining her composure after contemplating the laws and truths of Creation, Gaia felt reassured and refocused her attention to her immediate surroundings. She braced herself, watching as the volatile situation unfolded. Gaia could see everything that was happening everywhere in the universe at all times.

Uneek and Thunder were listening intently to Gaia's horrific account of what was happening on Earth, when

Thunder's long tail started twitching nervously.

Thunder's tail was his main defense against dangerous predators. The power of his tail became precariously evident as Thunder's rage surged to a heightened level spurred on by Gaia's warning of another possible extinction.

Today, however, the whipping action of Thunder's tail was not caused by an approaching predator per se, but rather, by a predator of a different sort - intense, emotional distress attacking his heart and soul.

Thunder's reaction was instinctual.

His discomfort and anger mounted as he listened to Gaia's revelations of carnage and disregard for nature by the human race. Some Earthlings were covertly aiding in the destruction of nature, disrupting Earth's ecosystem, for monetary gain.

Thunder could accept natural disasters, but those perpetrated on purpose were indefensible and inexcusable to him.

The more Gaia revealed to Uneek and Thunder, the angrier Thunder became. His emotions were expressed in his tail, an extension of his nervous system. Thunder was mad, mad as a hornet, as mad as an apatosaurus could possibly get.

Thunder had experienced an extinction once, the loss of his family, friends, his entire species. Gaia's story was striking a deep, emotional chord in his psyche, stirring up ageless, suppressed emotions of past, painful experiences.

Gaia was speaking from a deep place of despair. She knew though, that in the end, everything would be rectified. Any imbalances would be brought back into alignment. Nature would cleanse itself of any antagonistic elements in order to restore harmony to the ecosystem. Disrupting Gaia could lead to the removal of humankind from existence. The forces involved in self-preservation of Earth's natural systems were powerful, more powerful than Earthlings could comprehend.

Thunder's temper tantrum had continued to escalate, whipping at the air uncontrollably. The tantrum culminated in an abrupt and unbelievably loud crack of his tail, as it accidentally struck a nearby, well-established monster, an 80-foot-high oak tree. Its 10-foot-wide trunk snapped in half. The volume of Thunder's ear- shattering outcry was deafening. Uneek and Gaia instantly covered their ears in pain. They had watched the mighty oak fall through the surrounding trees, landing on the forest floor with an enormous crash.

Gaia and Uneek looked at each other in horror, trembling with gaping, open mouths, unable to speak. Uneek could see Gaia gasp, but couldn't hear her. They looked over at Thunder who was writhing in pain on the forest floor. He looked sullen, ashamed, and embarrassed as he licked the tip of his sore tail. He ventured a quick glance at Gaia and Uneek and just as quickly looked away again, away from their agonized faces.

Creeping low along the ground, he slowly made his way to the dying tree to lay down beside it. He carefully dragged his immense tail behind him, limp and throbbing with pain.

He proclaimed to the oak, "I am so sorry! I didn't mean to hurt you!"

He turned sadly to Gaia and Uneek saying, "I love trees! I love all nature!"

Lifting his head to scan the natural world around him, he said, "You are my world, and I couldn't live without you. "

Eventually Thunder looked back again at Gaia and softly uttered, "When you were telling us about the prevalent disregard for the Earth, the ecosystem, and our natural habitats, I became so enraged! It hurt me so badly to hear the truth, and now look at what I have done! I am just as bad as the money-hungry destroyers of our rain forests!"

He continued, "I apologize deeply for my rampage. It just brought back memories that had lain hidden inside me for I don't know how many millions of years, and I erupted like a volcano." He gently caressed the tree trunk, softly expressing his condolences.

Gaia looked over at Uneek, their hearing slowly returning, and whispered to him, "Suggest some serious anger management!"

CHAPTER 39

GAIA'S PROPOSAL

Gaia understood the time space time warp predicament and proceeded to share her wisdom of such matters with Uneek and Thunder.

She addressed Thunder, "You have entered into a space-time warp that has kept you suspended in time for 66 million years. You have been unable to progress to other natural dimensions in the space-time continuum. You've been imprisoned by a time warp where all progression came to an abrupt halt. You have been aimlessly wandering the continent looking for answers to your dilemma. You have 66 million years of learning under your belt, that you've gained from your relentless search for answers.

"You are invisible to all, except for just a few. I see you. Uneek sees you. Bright Wolf, the Wise One, who directed you to me could see you. The invisible veil which shrouds your existence is caused by the time warp which has placed you in a different dimension.

"The dimension you are trapped in is only accessible by those with greater intelligence and heightened consciousness, and who have the ability to understand universal dimensions. They can move freely from one to another.

"Some humans and animals have witnessed strange phenomena while being close to you: a sudden ripple in their own space time, a passing, visual blur, or an unexplainable, subtle feeling of eeriness in their energy fields. These are all natural occurrences, when different dimensions are close to each other.

"You have been manipulated into the space time warp by a superior, highly advanced intelligence. I don't know why this was done, but I believe that you have a higher purpose in a yet unknown scheme of things from an unknown origin.

"You have amassed a tremendous wealth of knowledge about the world while in the warp.

"You've been unable to die and pass on to embrace your next destiny. This was done to you on purpose to preserve you for some future reason.

"I also believe that meeting Uneek is part of the plan, as well as your appearance here before me, and your encounter with the Wise One.

"You must return to the home of your ancestors, Thunder. You must return to the lands that are known as the American Southwest. This is where you originally entered the space time warp 66 million years ago, and you must return there.

"I know this, but I can't tell you why you need to do this or what will happen to you when there.

"It is a long, long way for you to travel."

Turning to face Uneek, Gaia explained, "Uneek, you must accompany Thunder back to his ancestral home. You will be vital to the success of this journey. I don't know why, but you need to go with him to ensure his safe return."

Uneek and Thunder locked gazes for what seemed like an eternity, as they absorbed what Gaia had just revealed to them.

Thunder looked concerned, as he contemplated the implications of his journey home. Uneek was immediately willing and determined to help Thunder.

Uneek assuringly placed his hand on Thunder's lowered head and said, "Hey buddy. We'll be heading out West together. You have helped me out so many times. It is my turn now to reciprocate the shared goodwill of our friendship. I will help you get to where you need to go.

"You were the first one to befriend me, when I arrived on Earth. You have stood by me ever since. With your infinite knowledge, we made our way here. I think this was all part of our preordained destiny."

Thunder looked up at Uneek with a worried expression on his face, which displayed his reservations about embarking on another grueling, and perilous, cross-country trek.

He said to Uneek, "I don't think I can do this."

Uneek responded, "Sure you can, buddy! I'll be with you all the way. Let's make this happen! Besides, I have a couple of tricks up my sleeve!"

Thunder answered hesitantly, "Okay. I'll try to keep up with you."

Gaia looked pleased at their decision, and knew they were on the right path. But moreover, she was impressed by their unwavering friendship and mutual support for each other.

She signed with satisfaction and addressed them both. "Your time with me has resulted in a positive outcome, thanks to the willingness of both of you. You have been very receptive to my guidance and suggestions. I think the reason for your mission here has been accomplished.

"Thank you for stopping by, and know in your hearts and minds, that I am always here for you. Just look to nature, and the answers to all your questions will become clear. All you need to do is ask.

"Our time together must end now. I have a myriad of unexpected problems to deal with that require my attention. I leave you now with the best of wishes. You are both very special, and I wish you well." With that said, Gaia faded into the foliage, as she entered a different dimension.

Uneek and Thunder lingered for a while longer, feeling blessed by their encounter with the Mother of the Universe. Even though she had disappeared, they verbally thanked her over and over again, praising her for her patience, love, and words of wisdom.

They were momentarily amazed at a melodious reply emanating from deep within the forest. "I hear you. You're welcome."

Strangely, their awareness of the paranormal was somehow becoming more and more familiar to them, like a long, lost reality revealing itself and once again coming back to life.

Chapter 40
The Fight

Uneek understood everything that Thunder had shared with him. He had left his far away home to come here, fully equipped with basic knowledge of planet Earth. He was taught the nature of the solar system and all its planets and moons. He had been prepared with a scientific education of this part of the universe.

Known to be inhabited by humanoids, Earth was classified as hostile. It didn't even rank on the advanced scale of life forms. Earth and its inhabitants were still in the rudimentary, infant stages of evolution and development.

Technologically, with alien assistance, humans were slowly advancing closer to the Category I stage, but were still greatly lacking in social and spiritual development. The scope of impropriety was rampant, permeating every aspect of human life and behavior. Until they advanced to a stage of worldwide, peaceful harmony with each other, they would not be allowed to enter the cosmic social and technological order. They were still warlike and hostile even to each other.

Category I required achievement of human consciousness to a higher level of comprehensive, cosmic awareness, and relinquishing their weapons systems, especially those of mass destruction. Until then, they remained a hostile entity in the eyes of greatly advanced, higher intelligences in the universe.

Even given some of this knowledge beforehand, Uneek still had to learn more about the particulars of human social behavior. This is where Thunder's knowledge was instrumental and invaluable to him. It provided him an understanding of the human condition and the causes of the unrest and hostility.

After having listened to Thunder's lengthy tirade for days on end, Uneek realized that most of his observations were correct. Thunder had a good grasp of human behavior and the manmade systems that prevailed on Earth, despite being laced with anger and frustration. His subjective point of view was understandable given his present predicament and his past. He had taught Uneek so much.

Separating Thunder's negative and reactive feelings from his generously informative account, Uneek admitted to himself that Thunder had most of it right. Right on an Earth scale. He was lacking, though, in comprehension of the big picture. He had never been able to venture into the cosmos, having spent his entire existence grounded on Earth.

This is where Uneek could reciprocate and share his own vast knowledge and experiences in the cosmos. Thunder had taught Uneek so much about Earth, human behavior, and their prevailing manmade systems. Uneek would tell Thunder about the big picture, the aspects of the universe. Afterall, Uneek had an extensive, 12-million-year education and came from a nebular system billions of light years away.

Thunder had divulged to Uneek that he had seen off-world spaceships and knew that extraterrestrial life existed in the universe. His limited knowledge on this subject had been ascertained from observing the nature of a few alien spacecraft. This was just the tip of the iceberg, just an inkling of what the vastness of the universe held. These sightings had afforded him a small window into a universe of infinite possibilities. It was just a small peek into an otherwise hidden and secretive phenomenon.

Uneek had so much to share with Thunder. Maybe he could even 'show' Thunder the miraculous beauty of infinite space: maybe, sometime in the future, if ever possible. Uneek would love to reciprocate the learning aspect of their friendship.

Uneek turned his attention back to Thunder. He wanted to talk about their upcoming travel plans, the one subject that Thunder had so slyly avoided.

Uneek decided it was time to change the subjects that Thunder had been rambling on and on about for days now.

"You know buddy, we're heading out soon to begin our journey to the Southwest. We need to get some more shuteye, so we get refreshed and re-energized." Uneek had

Thunder in mind, when he said this, not himself. Thunder would need more rest and healing before embarking on this grueling quest.

"Oh, I had almost forgotten about that. Yes, that arduous prospect, looming in the recesses of my mind, stored in the "Trash" section of my brain."

"Thunder! We will need to start out early in the morning one day in the next couple of weeks. After some more restful nights, and after you eat and gain a little more weight. AND you need to stop talking incessantly into the wee hours of each morning, staying up all night. I'm still willing to continue listening to your experiences, but in a more controlled time span. You really need as much rest and healing that you can get before we head out again.

"But. But I don't think I can survive another journey like that again. Amarillo is over 1,200 miles from here! At 20 miles per day, my maximum speed, it would take me over 2 months to get there. I'm just not up for it. I don't think so!"

"Thunder. We've already traveled further than that on our way here from the East coast where we first met."

"Yes, I remember well. The slow, difficult journey here that took forever! Up the mountains, freezing my ass off! Then down the mountains, sliding most of the way down on my ass, slipping and sliding, scraping my butt on sharp, glacial boulders and rocks jutting up from the ground!

"Then the endless trudge through forests and farmlands, circumventing big cities, small towns, and people in general. That took twice as long and was twice as far!

"Then more mountains with miles and miles of trails that were too small and narrow for me! Squeezing through tight gaps in the rocky cliff sides, scraping my rib cage and chest all to hell just to make it through!

"Not to mention the tremendous toll it took on my legs, my muscles, my back! I need major physical therapy after what you've put me through!

"And my poor, sore feet! No amount of therapeutic pedicure therapy could rectify the damage done to my feet and nails. My feet were practically clawless from the wear and tear! It's taken months for them to grow back and look even half normal again.

"And all the damn power lines, barbed-wire fences, and hidden ruts and gullies! And the food along the way was shit! Leafless trees, baren bushes, frozen evergreens. And no water to be had from rock-hard, frozen rivers and lakes. I was absolutely famished and so thirsty, that my 15-foot-long throat felt like a desert, parched and dry. I had run out of saliva. It was literally hell on Earth!

"No, not again, not ever again, never, ever again! I'm done. Kaput! It has taken me months to recuperate and regain some semblance of my former self. I went from being a powerful, proud, dominant apatosaurus to a poor, downtrodden, beaten up, emaciated, and WEAK example of my species! I've lost over 3 tons of my brute weight!

No, I think you need to find a different traveling companion this time around."

"I have no reason to travel to the Southwest at all, other than to escort YOU there, safely and in one 'living' piece," retorted Uneek, thinking this was going to be a real bear getting Thunder to agree to go.

"Go without me! Just go. I'll stay here. I kinda like it here anyway. It's quite conducive to a comfortable lite style. The temperature works for me and there's unlimited vegetation. The water is clean and fresh."

"You know what Thunder? It's kind of ironic, that you would agree to this journey in front of Mother Nature, but then change your mind behind her back, when she's out of sight. You are a complete hypocrite! A coward! A liar, stubborn as all get-out, and you're wishy-washy to boot! No wonder they call you the 'deceptive lizard'!"

Thunder was taken aback, and Uneek thought he had gone too far, when he saw a tiny, agitated movement start up in the tip of Thunder's tail. But it was dark, and Uneek couldn't be sure. He decided to cool it.

Neither spoke for a long time, both gazing absent-mindedly into the fire.

They had never quarreled before, and this was a new, uncomfortable experience for both of them. A completely different dynamic had entered into their normally compatible, amiable friendship. They just sat silently pondering what to do, what to say, what to think.

CHAPTER 41

GAIA MAKES PEACE

Suddenly, a stealthy presence slowly made its way through the dark forest. As it came closer to the campfire, a figure became apparent, as it emerged from the shadows.

"Is there some kind of problem here?"

asked Gaia totally visible now.

Uneek jumped up to welcome Mother Nature, as Thunder recoiled, guilt-ridden with face reddening. He managed a weak, "Hello", returning again to the shelter of his own thoughts.

Gaia said, "I heard a tremendous ruckus of loud, angry voices enter my peaceful place a while ago. It was so disruptive to me and my work, that I decided to follow the source of the sounds and investigate. And lo and behold, I came upon you two again. Well, at least the disturbance has settled down, but why the long faces?"

Uneek looked over at Thunder, hoping he would answer Gaia's question, but to no avail. Thunder remained dismally quiet and somber, unwilling to divulge any information at all. A quick glance at his tail revealed that it had resumed a relaxed state, partially tucked under his hind quarters.

"Well, what's going on? You're both sitting there like dead fish." Thunder immediately thought about Barb.

Uneek got up and reached for a bundle of dry branches and twigs to stoke up the fire again, as the flames were slowly dying. As he did so, he looked at Gaia with sad, imploring eyes, but he still didn't utter a word.

153

"Hey guys. I'm going to make this as easy on you as I possibly can, since neither of you is stepping up to the plate.

"I heard every word that was said, even the exchange between you two before the altercation.

"My sense of hearing is extraordinarily acute to the point where I can pick up sound waves from miles away. I can even detect the identity of the source of the sound at those distances.

"You don't have to be afraid of divulging any information, since I already know exactly what happened. I know what was said, how it was said, and why it was said.

"So, we will start this conversation with an understanding that all three of us are on the same page. That way we don't have to rehash the whole, distasteful event, word for word, and we can move right on. Move forward to an honest, truthful conversation and understanding of the issues involved and hopefully come to a resolution. Understood?"

Both Uneek and Thunder were embarrassed but showed signs of compliance with Gaia's request. They felt more comfortable with the situation, as their adrenalin levels returned to normal. They both verbally and respectfully indicated their mutual consent.

With that settled, Mother Nature turned her attention to Thunder who was still sulking. "I can't imagine what you've been through, but I do know it must have been a lonely existence for you the past 66 million years. You've had absolutely no interaction with any other entity until just recently.

"For endless years, you've roamed aimlessly searching for answers with no one to share your ideas and thoughts with.

"You've lived all this time in total isolation with no way to bridge the gap between your dimension and those of others, who you can see, hear, and observe, but not communicate with.

"No interaction with anyone, because you don't even exist according to them. Such extreme isolation causes unfathomable emotional and mental states of loneliness and depression.

"Most would have gone insane within months with that amount of stress, but you have managed to persevere. You've remained lucid and unaffected by this ordeal for the most part, save a bit temperamental.

"You filled your lonely days and the hole in your heart by engaging in proactive, passionate learning.

"You've been able to fill your situation with an active mind. This has helped to sustain your sanity.

"You learned to be self-reliant, independent, and free to go and do as you please, because you had ro. You've been the king of your life, the lone king with no need to consider anyone else, when you need to make a decision.

"Yet, by observing the actions of those you saw, you've also developed a kind of one-way heart, a heart that feels for others, but at the same time, a heart that receives no love. You are an amazing creature that I am so honored to spend time with.

"But tell me, Thunder, what is it that truly gave you the drive, the impetus to go on, to conquer time and loneliness?"

Thunder thought about everything Gaia had just said to him. He closed his eyes and searched his soul for the answer to her question. He reached up into the ether with his spirit. He tried to find the right words to express the answer that was deep within him and simultaneously connecting him to the universe.

He replied, "I've always had faith in the Great Spirit, and an unwavering hope that I will eventually be saved from this plight. That this veil will be lifted from me, so I can finally be with the Great Spirit of the universe and all things again.

"I've always known that my dreams will come true. It's just a matter of time. The faith and hope I feel, bring such joy to my heart. I may not have had any interaction with others, but my heart is full of love that I have received from the Great Spirit. It comes to me even through the time warp. This love permeates everything in all dimensions. Nothing can hide or block the power of love or the direct connection with the Great Spirit. Not the time warp, not anyone or anything. The Great Spirit has created a fail-safe universe, infinite and eternal. It dwells in the universe and all things. There is no power greater, and it cannot be destroyed.

"Lesser powers have tried and still do, but it is impossible. This knowledge comes directly from the Great Spirit and is there for all to experience. It is free, but it is only accessible to those with pure hearts and minds. Otherwise, it cannot be understood or perceived.

"This is what has sustained me."

CHAPTER 42
RESOLVE

Both Mother Nature and Uneek felt the spirit that Thunder was sharing with them. Gaia then said, "In order to remove the veil that's upon you, you need to return home now. You have become used to having your own way, but now you have friends who are communicating with you and care for you, namely Uneek and me.

"I have told you what you need to do in order for your dreams to come true and finally get rid of the grip that this space time warp has on your body.

"You don't need to search any longer for answers. You have found them, and they have found you. The answers are right here.

"Knowing this, do you wish to continue living as you have, in endless limbo, or do you wish to move on, be unveiled and have all your dreams come true?

"Put this morbid, lonely existence behind you and return to where you belong.

"I know that Uneek has special powers and gifts, which he calls 'tricks.' He will be able to help you in ways we cannot begin to imagine. Trust him.

"You haven't had to trust anyone for a long time or had a friend since the time when your kind lived on this planet. He is your friend, and you can trust him with your life."

Looking over at Uneek, Mother Universe said, "Isn't that true, Uneek?"

The light had extinguished the sadness in his being, and he shined once again replying, "Yes."

Will you be able to make the journey back to his home easier for him to endure this time?"

Uneek again answered 'yes' to this question, and explained, "Just waiting for techno transmission with Uneek access.

"They are coming to me from billions of light years away, from my place of origin. My capabilities are about to be upgraded and enhanced. When I left my home nebula to come here, I was equipped with just the bare essentials for my own survival, not for the survival of anyone else.

"When Thunder and I embarked on the journey from the coast of South Carolina, I soon realized that Thunder needed additional help above and beyond my companionship, support, and encouragement.

"The journey was too treacherous for an apatosaurus. All I had to give him to help him fell way short of what was actually needed."

Thunder suddenly roused from his stubborn complacency, giving Uneek his undivided attention now. Mother Nature smiled to herself unnoticed by either.

Uneek fueled the fire again to keep Thunder warm. He said to Thunder, "I was so proud of you, and the way you tackled and overcame every obstacle on our way here. I knew you needed more help than I had to give.

"Somewhere in the wilderness of the Blue Ridge Mountains I realized this. I put in a special request for immediate technological assistance, for upgrades to enhance my capabilities here on Earth. I've been waiting for them to arrive ever since. It's been a month and a half now.

"According to my calculations of time, distance, and speed, the techno data pack should arrive any day now. I will feel it when it is downloaded in my mind. Then we can explore the new options and techno enhancements together. With our civilization's advanced technology, transmissions can be administered many times faster than the speed of light. Even at those incredible speeds, transmissions take time traversing such a long distance through space."

Uneek had Thunder's full attention. Thunder became totally engrossed in Uneek's disclosure and quickly asked during a pause, "What kinds of techno enhancements?"

Uneek, becoming more excited now, replied, "I'm not sure, but I requested powerful teleportation capabilities, including levitation and cloaking technology. Not sure what's on the way or what they sent. I won't know until I have it, but whatever they have sent will help us out on our trek to your home."

Thunder's reluctance to entertain the idea of more traveling was melting away, as Uneek described this new, promising development.

Uneek explained, "I didn't want to tell you until I was relatively certain that the transmission would be successful. I didn't want to raise your hopes prematurely. It's still not a 100% certainty, but it's close. Last night, I did some tracking research. The coordinates I entered to track the data package revealed that the transport had been recently 'escorted' through some massive, electromagnetic fields which were over 5 million light years in width. Then it had to circumvent a large number of huge, black holes lingering dangerously close to the mapped trajectory of the transport. I noticed that several course changes had been made by Space Command to ensure safe transport through these particular, problem areas. All looks good."

Mother Nature approached Thunder to ask the ultimate, make or break question, "Are you willing to take the trip now?"

Thunder, feeling much more reassured, peered over at his friend and replied indirectly to Gaia's inquiry by saying to Uneek, "Yes, I am! Beam me over, Uneek! Take me home, but, please, NOT down miles of country roads or through narrow, snow-covered mountain passes!"

PART 3

CHAPTER 43
THE RESTLESS UNIVERSE

In the eternal vastness of space, cosmic turbulence continued to occur as the natural phenomena of cyclical birth and death. Space dust and debris were compacted until the intense pressure erupted, birthing star systems, galaxies, and even new universes. Conversely in other parts of space, supernovae exploded and decompressed, leaving huge, black voids of powerful gravitational pull. Cosmic activity was ferocious.

During their lives, galaxies and stars collided with each other, pulled together by mutual, gravitational attraction. Eventually, the aftermath of these massive impacts was a period of settling back down into new and balanced states of peaceful homeostasis. Beautiful manifestations of intricate, life sustaining gardens came into being here and there in the calmer recesses of space. For a fleeting moment in time, life finally had its chance to exist and thrive in between the powerful episodes of dynamic, everchanging, and expanding universes.

This immeasurable expanse was the primordial soup of all that existed, that once existed, and that which didn't exist yet. Occasionally, it boiled and bubbled, throwing cosmic entities into and out of existence. Life inherently wanted to grow and expand, like the nature of the mother universe herself.

The cosmos was not confined to a cooking pot or any finite parameter. It had no boundaries, no constraints and was spreading outwardly in all directions and dimensions. Uneek wondered about whether or not his universe would eventually collide with another. He knew there were many universes, not only the one in which he was born. He was transfixed by contemplating the awesome wonders of nature. He realized that in his 16 million years of existence, he knew very little. He still had so much to learn, to explore, to experience, and his mind had no boundaries.

Uneek, however, also sensed an eerie uneasiness, a strange feeling of unnatural discord pervading the cosmos. He had received numerous updates from the CCL on the activities of the hostiles. Despite the intergalactic community's best efforts to defend benevolent civilizations from the hostiles, their forces continued to ravage and destroy many of them. Six more star systems along with inhabited planets had fallen, but only after they were pillaged of all warships, weapons, and raw materials. They were recruiting beings of these lost worlds to work for them by reconstructing their minds, ridding them of free will and instilling obedience. Their bodies were needed to work in the mines to recover valuable raw materials buried deep in planetary crusts and asteroids.

The last communique sent to him stated that the hostile forces were mustering their growing might into several factions on various fronts. The CCL assured all members that they were addressing these issues and to remain calm. Uneek thought that as the ongoing atrocities were continuously being committed, whatever the countermeasures that the CCL and intergalactic partners were executing, their actions were not very effective nor swift enough. Uneek had not been informed of their exact strategy. He realized that the benevolent civilizations had never encountered such a large insurgence of evil forces before, and were probably ill-equipped to defend against it. CCL members had joined in a mutual understanding to defend life, not to fight for it in an offensive way. Whatever the CCL was doing wasn't working in Uneek's opinion. Hostile aggression was proliferating throughout the universe, but Uneek was instructed not to get involved. He wouldn't sit back idly much longer, as entire civilizations were being destroyed. If the situation didn't improve soon, he would have to step in and do something. He didn't know what he could do, but he started considering his options. He had faith that the right course of action would reveal itself to him. The hostiles and their evil agenda had to be eradicated from existence, so that the natural harmony and peace in the universe could be restored.

CHAPTER 44
THE DATA PACKAGE

Miraculously, Thunder's ranting and raving had finally come to an end. There were no more sleepless nights of endless complaining. His mind was no longer plagued by thoughts of the past or by perturbing human issues. He seemed more hopeful and happier than Uneek had ever seen him.

The prospcct of heading West had now become Thunder's main objective. He made it a point to eat better and get more rest. His strength and enthusiasm were growing day by day. Uneek was relieved and pleased by the change in Thunder's attitude, and the positive energy he exhibited in the mornings, lasting all day long. He had done a 180.

The waiting, however, was difficult to bear. Several more weeks had passed, and the data package still hadn't arrived. Uneek and Thunder resigned themselves to remaining patient with passive submission to the inevitable, whatever that may bring.

When it finally came, both Uneek and Thunder were deep asleep under a canopy of Tennessee white oaks and sourwoods. The campfire was barely burning and smoldering. The air was thick and humid.

Uneek barely noticed the subtle influx of initial data, but as it intensified, he awoke with an internal jolt. He lay paralyzed, as the data was downloaded into his mind. It wasn't painful, only uncomfortable, but at the same time, astounding. His mind was bombarded with directed energy, releasing light beams of data, which were readily absorbed by receptors in Uneek's mind. The magnitude of the incoming data was almost

unbearable. Just when Uneek felt he could no longer endure its intensity, the process suddenly ended. He lay motionless, totally exhausted. After a few moments, he was able to sit up. He was glowing brightly, shining like a tiny version of the magnificent star that he was, but just a pinprick of bright light, only a spark of his true nature. He was aglow in the glory of his true essence which was hidden in an alternate dimension.

Uneek immediately diminished the intensity of his luminosity. He sat for a long time, pondering the implications of what had just happened to him. The data package had finally come and had been downloaded into his mind's system. The enormous amount of data he received was overwhelming. He was eager to explore the new options and abilities, wondering what enhancements had been given to him. He would delve into his mind to find out in the morning. As much as he wanted to do it now, he was much too tired from the experience to attempt any exploration at the moment.

He decided not to awaken Thunder. He would tell him the good news first thing in the morning. He got up and stoked the fire, watching as it regained a moderate level of heat to keep Thunder warm for the rest of the night. Uneek gradually dimmed out, completely drained. He fell asleep dreaming of super capabilities, like a space cadet.

CHAPTER 45
NEW ABILITIES

Uneek woke up extra early, brisk and rejuvenated after a short, but peaceful rest. He couldn't sleep any longer. He was excited, feeling like it was Christmas morning, and he couldn't wait to open his gifts. Thunder, still asleep, lay nearby snoring heavily.

Uneek began searching his mind for the mechanism that controlled his new capabilities. Finding it almost immediately, he noticed that it was different from what he was accustomed to. The options that he had normally used prior to receiving the data package, looked vaguely familiar to him, but had somehow changed. He remembered the capability that each option represented, but now they involved more levels and sublevels. The sublevels designated additional options to increase or decrease power and to determine scope. Panels opened up to enter required, detailed data for expansion and contraction, inclusion and exclusion, integration, engagement or disengagement, to name the major ones. Each sublevel had further sublevels which consisted of coordinate and astral grids, mapping options, and an enhanced universal positioning system or EUPS.

He also noticed a set of brand-new accessories which interested him the most. This new system in his mind seemed very complicated in comparison to what he was used to. The realm of possibilities had increased dramatically and could be applied to other entities, not only himself. Now he would be able to include Thunder in any options he chose. It would take him a while to learn how it all worked and to become proficient.

He envisioned the trials and errors that he would no doubt face. He would have to start out in small, incremental steps, like a newborn. But, in time, using this new system would become like second nature to him.

He looked over at Thunder and decided to let him continue sleeping. He went back into his mind to where he had seen the new capability options, and

which had initially sparked his interest the most. He perused the choices available to him and zoomed in on the levitation option. He surmised that since he could already levitate, this new option had been added to include others in its scope of operation, others like Thunder!

Uneek made his way to a clearing about 50 yards from camp. He was excited to explore this option first. He chose it and followed the prompts in the sublevels, until he felt sure of his responses and decisions, sure enough to try it. He scanned the object to be levitated and engaged the system. A huge, 4-ton boulder that he discovered in the meadow nearby suddenly rose ten feet from the ground and hovered in mid air for a few moments. Abruptly it dropped heavily to the ground. It landed with a loud thud, partially submerged in a huge hole. Uneek checked his inputs to figure out why the boulder hadn't remained in levitation mode. He found that he hadn't executed the sustained levitation option. However, he had learned something from his failed, initial attempt - how to lift objects and make them fall. This knowledge may come in handy sometime in the future.

Uneek continued to levitate objects, mainly boulders, that he found in the meadow, until he had perfected the ability. He even learned to lift several boulders at the same time, and was able to lower each one back to the ground gently. This was fun! He let many just drop in a heap, while he levitated others to heights of over 100 yards in the air! He levitated a bunch of rocks and flung them all around the meadow. He had mastered levitation along with forward movement. He had this down pat and felt triumphant at his success. After several hours, he returned to camp, where he found Thunder still asleep. Uneek stared at the sleeping giant, and his wheels started turning.

Suddenly, Thunder's body rose several inches from the ground and remained suspended in the air! The movement of Thunder's body upward was so subtle, that it didn't even disturb his sleep. He hovered, snoring away to his heart's content. Uneek was so amused at the sight of Thunder floating, that he could barely stifle the urge to burst out loud! It was hilarious! From past experiences, Uneek had felt that same tickle of hilarity, especially in places where he was expected to be quiet, obedient, and respectful, like in Space Counsel meetings or spiritual training classes. The more somber the atmosphere, the funnier the situation would become. At times, he literally had to excuse himself from the premises to keep from bursting out loud and disrupting the entire congregation.

An ornery being could have a heyday with this capability, but Uneek was not the ornery type. He had not expected that this option would work so easily with his newly acquired knowledge of commands and the data coordinates he had entered. He was elated that it worked so well, and that he had made the correct decisions on the control panel. He could hardly wait to tell Thunder and demonstrate what he could do. But for now, he lowered Thunder gently back down to his original position on the ground and let him continue sleeping. This gave him a little more time to check out some of the other available options.

While he was still sleeping, Thunder suddenly shrunk down to the size of a pea and then totally disappeared and reappeared again! Thunder hadn't noticed any of this.

Uneek chose "Teleport" and reviewed the sublevels involved. He and Thunder would definitely have to try that one out. If all went well, he could take Thunder directly to Amarillo, Texas in the blink of an eye, or slowly travel in levitation mode, if they wished to enjoy the sites on Earth below. He mused to himself. Maybe he would even take Thunder on a journey to outer space and show him his world!

Uneek played around with all the options, until he felt comfortable with their meanings and required data inputs. He stopped only when he noticed Thunder was beginning to stir. Uneek waited patiently for Thunder to wake up on his own. It was midmorning, and hunger pains would soon rouse Thunder to full consciousness. Yawning and sucking in a huge amount of oxygen, Thunder slowly opened his enormous eyes. Sunlight draped over him like a blanket. Uneek knew he would head straight for the tree line and nearby stream to quench his thirst with a long drink of cool water. Uneek greeted him with, "Good morning."

"Morning," was the reply. He slowly lifted his massive body, stretching his huge limbs and started moving slowly toward the trees for breakfast and a drink.

Uneek yelled out after him, "Hey! When you're done, come back here. I have something important to share with you." Thunder barely heard a word that was said, as he beelined his way to the edge of the woods.

Chapter 46
Sharing the News

Thunder eventually returned to camp, fat and satisfied. Uneek was eagerly waiting for him and asked, "How was your breakfast? "

"Scrumptious!" Thunder replied.

Thunder looked at Uneek with a puzzled expression on his face. He said, "Something weird happened, though. After eating my fill of leafy branches in the woods, I decided that it was time for dessert, so I made my way to the meadow in search of berry bushes. Strangely, I noticed a whole bunch of huge boulders half submerged in the soil like they had fallen out of the sky! Did I miss something?"

Uneek laughed and said, "You sure did! That was my doing. I received the data package last night and was practicing all morning with levitation, teleportation, and a number of other abilities I now possess. I need to show you my new skills, and we need to start practicing them on you. We can finally start planning our trip out West!"

"What do you mean? Practice on me?"

Uneek replied, "Yes! We need to practice levitating and teleporting together, so we'll be ready to take off when the time comes." Uneek did not share any of the errors he had made while learning.

"No way! Definitely not! I saw those boulders stuck deep in the ground! Looks like you miscalculated and dropped them! Uneek! I am not made of stone! I am flesh and blood, and if you were to drop me, I wouldn't survive the impact. I could end up a 20-ton mound of squish!"

Uneek laughed inwardly but understood Thunder's reservations and reluctance. Uneek explained, "We'll start out small, Thunder, and build our way to full competence. I've been practicing since dawn and can show you what I've learned so far. I wouldn't jeopardize your life in any way. Granted, I need to learn more about some of these other enhanced options, but I feel confident about utilizing the ones I mentioned. We will work together on this to ensure your safety and build your confidence. Before long, you'll be begging me to take you up. Trust me. I have complete faith in our technology. Besides, the data package was designed especially for you."

"Yeah. You love me like a rock! I saw those boulders embedded in makeshift graves with my own eyes!"

"Most of them were dropped on purpose," Uneek explained.

Uneek held Thunder's attention firmly in his gaze and gently lifted him up about 10 inches. The extent of the levitation was so subtle that Thunder didn't even feel it and was totally unaware that he was hovering above the ground. It wasn't until Uneek averted his gaze, that Thunder looked down and realized he was not on the ground but floating above it.

"Put me down right now, dammit!" he screamed in terror. Uneek lowered him back to the ground with an imperceptive movement. Thunder was scared and angry even after he was standing again on all fours, unhurt. He pretended to have ill effects from being lifted and feigned dizziness by stumbling around like a drunk for a few minutes. It didn't work.

Uneek ignored the show and said, "See. That wasn't so bad, was it?"

Still panting, Thunder yelled, "Please! Let me know ahead of time before you ever do anything like that again! You scared the bejeebers out of me!"

Uneek knew that it would take some time and plenty of patience to get Thunder to the point where he felt confident and comfortable with Uneek at the helm. It took another two weeks until Thunder had acclimated himself to trust in Uneek's technological skills. Many long days were spent practicing, gaining trust, until they actually started making plans. Uneek was right, though. Before long, Thunder was pleading with Uneek to take him higher and higher into the atmosphere. He was actually beginning to enjoy this mode of transportation, moving so easily and feeling as light as a feather. Uneek was overjoyed by Thunder's progress and began to plot out the course of their upcoming venture.

CHAPTER 47

UNEEK GOES TO WAR

This was not the only trip that Uneek was planning to undertake. The CCL had relayed vital information concerning the locations of various factions of hostile presence, reigning terror throughout neighboring areas of the cosmos. A significant force was indicated, traveling between the Andromeda and Milky Way Galaxies. It was headed toward a part of the Virgo cluster where a large number of inhabited planets existed.

Another huge fleet of warships was spotted in the Taurus sector. It loomed stealthily in the Crab Nebula near the Pleiades. A third major front was roaming through the region of Orion. The CCL was busy notifying the vast number of civilizations in these quadrants, warning of the impending threat that the hostile forces imposed. In response, many geared up for the possibility of war. The future looked grim, as the hostile power grew stronger with every conquest.

Uneek's desire to confront the dire situation grew stronger, too. He had formulated a plan of action in the back of his mind. He couldn't stand by and be complacent any longer. The exact plan had begun as an idea in a recent dream. It continued to take shape and eventually evolved into a viable strategy. His final decision would involve stealth, courage, and formidable action. He couldn't divulge his intentions to anyone, not the CCL, not Thunder, not anyone. His plan was beyond the echelons of secrecy.

Uneek had the arduous task of informing Thunder that he would be gone for a while. Of course, Thunder would want to know why, where, when, what, and with whom.

He would have to keep it simple. Uneek explained to Thunder that he was going on a secret mission for a few days. To Uneek's surprise, the only question that Thunder asked was, "What about the campfires at night? Who's going to manage that for me?"

Uneek responded, "You don't need them now. It's become so hot and humid. Even the nights are sweltering. It's the middle of summer! You'll be fine. I'll be back before you know it."

Uneek was relieved that Thunder's only concern was the fires he started up every night. Thunder respected the term "secret" and did not prod Uneek for any additional information. Deep down he knew that it wasn't the campfires that Thunder worried about. In actuality, he was going to miss him, the long talks they had every evening, and the realization that he would be alone to fend for himself. Thunder was not high maintenance, but as independent as he was, he had grown accustomed to Uneek's presence. It was also apparent that Thunder harbored a foreboding sense of fear for Uneek's safety. The one question that Thunder had asked held all these feelings which were disguised in the flames of campfires.

That night Uneek did not build the usual fire. Thunder realized he was warm enough without one. They spent the evening talking about the Virgo, Orion, and Taurus Constellations, while pointing them out individually in the night sky. Using his hologram generation capability, Uneek enlarged the image of the North America Nebula in the Cygnus Constellation with laser directed light beams so it could be seen by Thunder. Uneek showed him the resemblance the nebula had to the shape of North America.

He pointed out the brightest star, Deneb, to the right. He told Thunder that what he was seeing was over 1,600 light years away. Thunder was full of questions, and Uneek accommodated him with detailed answers as best he could, sharing all he knew, or at least all that Thunder could possibly comprehend.

Thunder stared at two distinct stars that appeared close together, and Uneek explained that in reality, they were light years apart from each other. Uneek said, "The star to the left just appears to be next to the other one, but in reality, it is a much bigger, a red giant. Because it is so distant, it appears to be the same size as the other smaller star. Uneek went on to explain some of the aspects of the true nature of the cosmos and that

it existed as a dimensional entity. The panoramic view of stars and other heavenly bodies did not exist on a flat two-dimensional plane as represented in astronomical charts and maps. In addition to width and length, the dimensions of depth and time existed. It was a matter of cosmic dimensional perspective versus linear perception. Uneek knew more dimensions existed but didn't want to cause any further confusion. Thunder nodded with apparent understanding. Uneek finally abated Thunder's curiosity by saying, "The cosmos is much more complex than it appears on paper or with the naked eye. I'll show you this one day when I take you on a journey to outer space." Thunder was satisfied with that prospect as their exploration of the night sky came to an end.

"I'll be leaving at dawn before you wake up," Uneek said.

"Have a safe trip," Thunder replied, hiding his face. "Good night, and thanks for all your inspiring stories about the star systems. The universe sounds incredibly beautiful, and it will be exhilarating to experience. Can you take me up and show me sometime soon?"

"I certainly will after I come back." Uneek could tell even from the back of Thunder's head that he was grinning from ear to ear.

Uneek spent the rest of the evening going over his plan. The exact coordinates of the last-known hostile locations had been provided along with the warning sent by the CCL. This information would prove vital to him.

Uneek was up before dawn. Thunder was sleeping like a log. Brimming with conviction and determination, Uneek engaged the cloaking system and teleported into deep space.

Chapter 48

Uneek's Splendor

Uneek teleported to a largely empty space in the vicinity of Virgo close to where hostiles had been congregating. They were heading to a planet -rich area of the constellation, no doubt to orchestrate their next attacks. They were still light years from their destination, when Uneek spotted them. He waited to make sure that the hostile force was in a relatively empty area of the cosmos. Undetected, Uneek made his way toward them and centered his tiny, cloaked spark in the very middle of the hostile armada. He had never seen such a huge fleet of warships in one place in his entire life. Arrogant and self-assured by their ominous might, the hostiles were intent on perpetrating their next series of attacks.

Uneek glanced at Spica, the brightest star in Virgo, and suddenly yearned to shine once again like the beautiful star he actually was. Uneek emerged from his obscure dimension in the full glory of his true being, a gigantic blue star 47 times the magnitude of the yellow Sun star of Earth. In a milli-second he flashed in and back out of the two dimensions. He shone in his magnificent splendor, as a tremendous body of incredible heat and fusion. Uneek engulfed the entire hostile fleet inside his body, and it was blasted out of existence in an instant. No words could describe Uneek's power and the destructive effect he emanated. There had been no time for the fleet to warn the other hostile regiments, lurking near Orion and Taurus. Not a trace of the destroyed force or any residual evidence remained of the enormous hostile war front. They had been obliterated to nothingness.

His small spark, brimming with the light of victory, Uneek wasted no time. Making sure his spark was cloaked, he teleported to Orion's Belt. He stopped at a short distance from the belt of the Three Kings, Alnitak, Alnilam, and Mintaka, shining brightly before him. He imaged they were his stellar audience and could have sworn that they acknowledged him! Many a stellar friend had perished at the dreadful hands of the hostiles.

He checked his Universal Positioning System (UPS) and input the CCL coordinates of the last known hostile location in this part of the cosmos. Tracking their movements, he saw them immediately. He zeroed in on them using his powerful telescopic vision. Cautiously he entered into their fleet and followed alongside them totally unaware of his presence. They were headed further into an area of empty space on their way to the Flame Nebula, with Its innumerable stellar systems and thousands of planets. At the most opportune time in space, Uneek once again burst forth into the hostile dimension, reducing the immense fleet of hostile warships to an empty void. At unfathomable velocities, rouge, intergalactic stars seemed to wink at him as they streaked by.

Uneek carefully studied the location of his final target, roaming toward the Taurus Constellation, home to the Hyades and Pleiades star clusters. Uneek reverted back to his customary spark, moving the bulk of his body back into the alternate dimension. He cloaked his spark and teleported to Taurus, where he would rid the universe of the last, surviving regiment of evil forces.

Uneek knew many more hostiles existed throughout the cosmos, but they were sparse and fragmented. Most had joined the hostile fronts, and soon they would all be destroyed along with their treacherous leaders. Any hostiles that remained were scattered and would be unable to cause much destruction. They would be far and few between. They would lack the armaments, organization, and leadership needed to further their evil agenda. They would have to hide for the rest of their lives.

CHAPTER 49
THE LAST ANNIHILATION

Uneek saw the distant hostile space force speeding toward the Hyades nebula. Unaware of the fates of their partners, they moved forward in unison, confidently and with the darkest of intensions. Uneek merged easily into the hostile convoy without detection, as they traveled toward the planet-rich star cluster. Reaching an area of open space, Uneek could safely turn into his natural state without causing collateral damage. He prepared to enter the hostile dimension full-bodied.

Uneek took another look around before executing his final act of destruction. To his surprise and dismay, he noticed a secondary hostile force in the far distance, coming around from behind the star cluster! The hostiles planned their attack from two fronts! He immediately refrained from deploying his initial plan. He pondered this new development, as he cruised among the hostile warships.

After attacking their intended targets in the Hyades nebula, the unified hostile forces would no doubt head toward the Pleiades. Uneek had to reconsider and readjust his strategy. He couldn't annihilate both forces at the same time. He had to choose which one to destroy first. He tried to figure out how to do this without drawing attention to himself and alerting the remaining force. Uneek stealthily withdrew from the convoy and headed toward the secondary force which had migrated to a position behind the opposite side of the nebula. When Uneek neared the force, he confronted a massive armada of a thousand warships, many of which seemed strangely familiar to him. Some were the same warships confiscated from Crossroads and Selica! The hostile forces had finally emerged from their hiding place in the asteroid base in deep space! The front he was facing consisted of the most elite, superior, advanced starships ever built. Uneek felt a sudden pang of impending remorse, as he approached these magnificent ships, knowing he was about ready to destroy them.

Unbeknown, he matched their velocity and moved secretly into the center of the convoy. His magnitude increased to its fullest extent, as he entered their dimension. The entire hostile force was vaporized in a fraction of a second. His sudden appearance as a huge, blue star would have appeared as a natural phenomenon of the star nebula. The collaborated communications between the two hostile forces had come to a sudden, mysterious end, and all went silent. The remaining fleet was alarmed, causing widespread suspicion and panic. Uneek watched as they abruptly fled, scattering in all directions, like fireworks. The retreating ships eventually fizzled out, disappearing into the darkness.

Uneek predicted that this would happen. He was content with the fact that he had rid the world of at least one of the two. He had reduced the evil, alien forces to a more manageable level. The CCL and intergalactic forces could now root out and destroy any remaining hostiles.

The universe already felt more peaceful to Uneek, and the eeriness of evil that had pervaded the cosmos was gone. In time, civilizations would return once again to harmonious coexistence. Uneek glanced over at the Pleiades star cluster where his friends were. They were safe. He would bring Thunder here and introduce him to the Seven Sisters, who would welcome him with open beams of light.

Uneek's work was done. He left the Taurus sector with satisfaction and teleported back to Earth. He had made a difference. The uneasiness in his heart and mind had dissipated. It would take time for civilizations to realize that there was no longer an evil, alien threat looming in the universe.

Uneek would never divulge what had happened. He did not crave the limelight or the accolades that would have come his way, if he disclosed what he had done. He remained silent. Inwardly, he enjoyed peaceful happiness and personal bliss. This is what differentiated him from the status quo and made him unique.

CHAPTER 50
RETURN TO THUNDER

Uneek sat watching Thunder as he slept. Snoring loudly, his enormous chest heaved up and down, as he inhaled and exhaled. It was already past noon, but Thunder didn't stir. Wasn't he hungry? Several more hours passed before Thunder woke and moved lethargically toward the trees along the stream. What was "wrong with him?" Uneek thought. After an usually short meal, he returned to the cold campfire and resumed a supine position, falling asleep again.

It was late afternoon, and Uneek began to worry. He had to let Thunder know he had returned. He knew better than to try tickling Thunder's monstrous nose, so Uneek began softly humming the familiar, Seven Sisters' tune. There was no response to his melodious song. Uneek gradually increased the volume until it reached a deafening roar. Thunder reared up and screamed so loudly, the ground shook. "What the hell?!"

Blurry-eyed, Thunder tried to focus. Uneek noticed a glint of deep sadness in his eyes, when Thunder's gaze finally came to rest on him. "I'm back," Uneek said.

Thunder retorted, "What in hell were you trying to do? Blast out my eardrums?"

Smiling, Uneek simply replied, "Just trying to wake you up to let you know I am here."

Extremely irritated, Thunder huffed indignantly, "I HATE alarm clocks! That was hellaciously LOUD!"

"It worked, didn't it? Waking you up is like trying to revive a dead corpse!" Uneek laughed and was glad to see Thunder in this ill-tempered state. He was going to be okay.

Uneek asked, "How have you been doing? What have you been up to, besides snooping around in tree canopies and sleeping?"

Settling down, Thunder replied somberly, "Not much of anything. You were gone a lot longer than I anticipated."

That look of deep sadness returned to Thunder's eyes. He said, "I started believing you were never coming back."

Somehow Uneek realized that Thunder was suffering from a bout of separation anxiety. He had spent all his time sleeping with only an occasional trip to the woods to nibble. He had lost some weight.

"Of course, I was coming back. My mission just took a little longer than I thought it would."

"After the first few days that you told me you would be gone, the time turned into a week, then two weeks. I thought you had left forever, or worse, that something bad happened to you. How did everything go with your mission?"

Uneek replied, "All went well. Mission accomplished!"

The late afternoon turned into early evening. It became a little chilly, so Uneek built a warm, inviting fire that soothed Thunder's mood. Thunder smiled for the first time since his return. Thunder explained that it had rained heavily the night before, as a cold front came through. He was warming up, both in body and attitude. Any remnants of separation anxiety had dissipated.

They spent the evening talking about all the places Uneek had visited while he was gone, but carefully avoided any mention of what he had actually done.

Uneek said, "I have been planning our trip itinerary for when we head out West. We'll make our way to Amarillo, Texas first. We can teleport most of the way. I thought we could occasionally levitate, so we can take in some of the sites along the way. We'll spend a few days northeast of Amarillo and camp by Lake Meredith. You can swim and float around in the lake to your heart's content. It is a recreational area with lots of trees and great vegetation. We will need to remain cloaked while we are there."

Thunder cheered up and chimed in, "When are we heading out?"

"After a little more practice in teleporting and levitating, AND after you fatten back up a little," Uneek answered.

Thunder said, "I'm excited to finally go. We've been here in Tennessee for a long time. I'll eat better and put on the weight I lost. Then I'll be ready to go!"

Uneek added, "And exercise your monstrous legs! You've been inactive for weeks!"

Thunder was agreeable to all these prerequisites. However, he asked nervously, "Why the leg exercises? I won't have to do any walking, will I?"

"Hardly any at all. Just a little bit."

Thunder peered at Uneek suspiciously and asked, "Just a little bit?"

Uneek reassured him that that was correct. Satisfied with the response, Thunder settled himself into a comfortable sleeping position, as Uneek stoked the fire. Tonight would be a night of good rest for both Thunder and him, the best they'd had in weeks.

Thunder turned toward Uneek and told him, "I'm glad you're back."

Uneek sighed, "So am I. Good night, my friend. Sleep well."

Uneek spent the next few hours regrouping from the stresses incurred by his precarious mission. He checked for any word from the CCL, but there was none. Thunder was safe and sound asleep, snoring like a mini tornado.

The universe had returned to its normal, dynamic self with the annihilation of the hostile threat. All was well now with the world. Therefore, all was well with him, too. Uneek remained awake for a few more hours, going over the plans for their upcoming trek. He fell into a deep sleep after spending weeks with none.

CHAPTER 51
UNEEK'S IDEA

Uneek awoke with an idea that came to him in the dream he had the night before. He performed a complete scan of Thunder. He then interrogated his enhanced Universal Positioning System for the origin of the dimension in which Thunder was imprisoned. He also sought for the exact location of the space time warp when it was originally created. The results of the query came back with a distinct dimensional signature, but no findings were given on the space time warp other than its present-day location. The system was not understanding the question, or else he wasn't asking the right one. The UPS's only response was a static-like, electronic blur. Maybe his line of questioning was too vague, requiring more specific data variables and tighter parameters. But first, Uneek reviewed the results that he did get - namely, the dimensional signature. At least, the system had identified the dimension Thunder was stuck in.

The results indicated a prevalent dimension in an alternate universe, stemming from a source in the direction far beyond the region of Cassiopeia. Just the fact that the system recognized the dimension was a starting point. Uneek could expand on this information and adjust the data to a more focused set of inquiries. Uneek figured he had to specify a past derivative of time other than the present. In addition, he had to reduce the scope of the possible location in space at that particular time. Uneek was trying to find out Thunder's whereabouts when the warp became effective. Hopefully, Uneek would be able to obtain some useful data that would help them, instead of wandering aimlessly around the Southwest. Uneek set the time variable to circa 65,998,000 BCE. He then input the latitude and longitude coordinates for the entire area around the Four Corners which included Arizona, New Mexico, Wyoming, and Colorado. Uneek added this data to the dimensional signature along with the secret Akashic Records. He anticipated that the convergence of this particular set of criteria would work and lead to a positive match. Uneek executed the search for analysis.

Suddenly and unexpectedly, the exact location revealed itself in Uneek's mind, shining like a beacon of light. With the location they sought permanently fixed in Uneek's mind, he and Thunder could now make their way to the Bisti/De-Na-Zin Wilderness Badlands in northwestern New Mexico. The path to Thunder's freedom became crystal clear, no longer obscured in a mist of uncertainty.

CHAPTER 52

THE CONUNDRUM

Teleporting to Amarillo went smoothly without a hitch. Thunder enjoyed traveling periodically in levitation mode, where he could see all the features of the landscape from his lofty, vantage point. Uneek eventually guided them to a secluded cove at Lake Meredith, northeast of Amarillo. Thunder had his moments wading and floating in the lake, while Uneek worked on delineating the journey to their next stop. He shared the discoveries and results of his inquiries with Thunder, who had returned to the beach after an early morning swim. Refreshed and eager to find out where they were heading next, Thunder settled in next to the smoldering campfire. Uneek presented his plan to Thunder, telling him that they would be on their way to the Farmington, New Mexico region. They would start out early the following morning.

Thunder asked, "Why Farmington?"

"The Bisti Badlands are only 43 miles south from there, and that is where you were encapsulated by the warp long ago. We will establish our base camp near Farmington," Uneek replied.

"Why not camp right in the badlands?" Thunder objected.

"You couldn't survive a single day in the badlands. Temperatures can climb to over 115 degrees Fahrenheit in the summer months. The badlands are located in an extremely dry, arid desert. There is no water for you to drink and no vegetation for you to feed on either. You would dehydrate within a few hours and pass out, shriveling up like a mega raisin, sun-dried. We will have to make small excursions in and back out of the badlands every two or three hours. We'll camp in a more amiable habitat, maybe near the Navajo Reservoir, which is close by, only 34 miles east of Farmington. There is a dam there that blocks part of the Colorado River, creating a beautiful, manmade lake. Plenty of water, to drink and swim in and vegetation to satisfy your humongous appetite. That's where we will go tomorrow."

"Sounds like a terrific plan!"

Thunder blurted out.

"We'll look for the original spot in the badlands, where you were placed in the space time warp. I know exactly where it is in my mind. I can sense it. It is beckoning to me, disclosing the location. We'll still have to explore the area for it, and you will be doing a minimal amount of walking. I'll teleport us as close as I can, as I follow the beacon. We'll still have to do a little hunting. There is no map or any signs that mark the spot. That's why I had to convert the location in my mind to Earth coordinates, so I can apply them to the actual landscape. That will help us navigate to the badlands," Uneek explained.

"I see.", Thunder snorted agreeably, even though he didn't have a clue as to what Uneek was talking about.

Thunder stood at the base of a gigantic red, sandstone rock formation that rose upward hundreds of feet into the sky. He and Uneek found themselves surrounded by strange, shaped megaliths, buttes of red, oxidized iron mountains and hoodoos, jutting up like monstrous spikes from the desert floor. Honed by eons of wind and water erosion, they presented an eerie site that neither had ever experienced before. Boulders and sedimentary flows had been deposited here long ago by rivers and glacial run-off from nearby mountains. The buttes and spires were a testament to the passage of time. They studied the stratified layers that the sedimentary flows left over millions of passing years. The austere landscape surrounding them looked completely alien to Uneek and Thunder, as they viewed the threatening, harsh reality of the badlands. They were amazed at the geological significance of recorded events, preserved and etched in the rock formations.

"This place is awful!" Thunder uttered in disbelief.

"Are you sure you don't want to camp here tonight?", Uneek taunted.

Ignoring him, Thunder stared at a distant butte that resembled the head of an apatosaurus. He pointed it out saying, "Look at that strange rock formation! It's a sign. We're close."

Uneek could sense the beacon pulsating in his mind, but for some reason, the real-world location eluded him. They had teleported straight here from the lake, but no clear path opened up to him, that they could follow from here. Uneek's attention was continuously drawn to the sand of the desert floor in front of him.

Uneek finally asked Thunder, "Do you feel anything? Any vibrations, anything familiar to you? I know we are in the correct area. My beacon is confirming that."

Thunder replied hoarsely, "All I feel is that I'm hot as hell and my throat is getting parched! This dry heat is unbearable! I can't take it much longer. My body temperature is way too high. I need shade and water! Please Uneek! Get me out of here! This place is killing me!"

Uneek realized they had to leave right away, before Thunder passed out.

"Okay, Thunder. We'll head back to the lake."

Before teleporting back to the Navajo Reservoir, Uneek had an uncanny sensation as he stared, fixated on the same spot in the sand. His curiosity flared brightly, as he focused on the signal, emanating from the center of his mind. He tore himself away from the perplexing conundrum and teleported back to their campsite at the lake with Thunder securely by his side. It seemed they had hit a dead end. There was nothing there, even though his mind said there was.

Chapter 53

Fortitude

Uneek and Thunder arrived instantaneously at the lake. Thunder dragged himself directly into the cool, fresh water, which was shaded by forest trees along the lake shore. He remained in the lake for an extraordinarily long period of time, exhausted and spent from their trip to the badlands. His temperature slowly dropped back down to a comfortable level, and Uneek knew Thunder would be fine.

Uneek rehashed what had happened in the badlands over and over again in his mind. Why was his mind drawn into the sand below him whenever he zeroed in on the beacon's signal? He was determined to find the answers. It didn't make sense.

Thunder eventually returned to camp after leaving the lake and stopping for a quick snack. He plopped down next to where Uneek would be building a fire for the night.

Uneek asked, "Are you feeling any better?

Thunder replied, "Yes, I am, but I'm so tired. The badlands pooped me out. I have to rest now." He closed his eyes and before long fell fast asleep.

While Thunder slept, Uneek was impelled to figure things out. He tenaciously attempted to resolve the problematic issues facing him by venturing into his mind and the historical archives of the Bisti badlands. He went over everything with a fine-toothed comb, but so far nothing explained the paradox and the odd fixation he had experienced with the sand, drawing him in. He explored the geological history in relation to the current topography. He remembered Thunder's stories about the

195

shallow sea basins that he, his fellow apatosauruses, and all the other life forms of his time enjoyed. Thunder had always told him he came from a land of paradise. Why was the beacon in his mind pointing to the Bisti badlands? They sure weren't the land of paradise that Thunder talked about. The whole thing baffled Uneek.

Uneek kept returning to the sand. He knew that sand indicates that at some time in the past, the land must have been covered by water, a sea or ocean. This was the same case with the desert sands of the badlands. Where did the water disappear to? Then Uneek discovered from the archives that the current elevation of the badlands was over 5,400 feet above sea level! Suddenly, Uneek understood why the beacon was signaling from beneath the sand. The spot where Thunder had entered the space time warp was over a mile underground from where they had just been! It was under their feet all along! Sixty-six million years ago, what was now the Bisti Badlands, was land at sea level! It boiled down to a matter of time in conjunction with tremendous geological changes! Uneek stuck to this line of thought. He was on to something.

He found out that in prehistoric times, the Western Interior Seaway covered a large area of North America, extending from the Gulf of Mexico northward all the way to the Arctic Ocean. The continent was literally divided in half by this enormous seaway, separating the West coast's Cordilleran land mass from the East Coast's Appalachian land mass. After immense subduction events in the middle of the continent, the forces of tectonic plate movement caused the whole area to sink and become inundated by water from the Gulf of Mexico. This was the shallow sea that existed during the time when Thunder lived! Uneek was beginning to get excited by the revelations that were unfolding. He was beginning to figure it out, little by little.

He wanted to know what happened to the seaway. He discovered that the western Farallon Plate had continued the subduction process deep underneath the North American Plate, causing tremendous heat and uplifting of the Earth's crust. Over the expanse of millions of years, plate tectonics caused the Earth's mantle and crust to rise up over a mile. The seaway eventually ran off the elevated plateau and dissipated.

Now that he had solved the mysterious location of the warp origin, a bigger challenge presented itself to him. How in the world was he going to be able to help Thunder return to a location one mile underground? He would have to sleep on that one. He was worn out by all this mental activity and started getting tired. If he was lucky, maybe he would have a miraculous dream tonight that revealed the answer.

He put a couple of dry logs on the dying fire. The nights out here could get quite cool, and he had to keep Thunder's body temperature regulated. He took a look at Thunder and thought to himself, "I will find a way, friend. We WILL set you free!" Uneek's strength of mind would guide him to the solution. With his mind still whirling from all the questions and possibilities, Uneek started humming. It was just the thing to ease his rampant thoughts and smooth out the raw edges of psychic overdrive.

Chapter 54

Journey to the Pleiades

When morning came, Uneek was surprised to see Thunder already bathing in the lake. He had slept about half the day before and all night. Noticing that Uneek was awake, Thunder came out of the water and lumbered toward him, sputtering to himself. As he approached, Uneek could clearly hear what he was grumbling about.

"I'm never going back there again!", Thunder exclaimed. "It's not exactly my cup of tea!"

Uneek loved being around Thunder, while he was in one of his cantankerous moods. Jutting in, Uneek reassured him, "You don't have to, ever again. Don't worry. That was quite a harrowing experience for you! You seem to have recovered nicely, though. Your cheeks are nice and rosy again. You were as pale as the moon yesterday. You're back to your grumpy self again! Good morning!" Thunder stared open-mouthed at Uneek but didn't say another word about it. He just replied with a weak greeting of his own, "Morning."

Uneek went on to bore Thunder for the next hour with all the details of what his research had brought to light. Uneek ended with, "I think we need a break. Would you like to take a journey to the Pleiades with me and meet the Seven Sisters?"

Thunder jumped up enthusiastically, his tail wagging heavily from side to side on the ground. He screamed out loud with joy, "Oh yes! I have been waiting so long and so patiently for you to ask but didn't dare bring it up. I knew you would come through. When can we go?"

"Settle down. Your tail is creating a trench in the dirt!" Thunder immediately stopped moving his tail and sat up waiting for a reply.

"We can go today if you'd like. I miss the Sisters and am eager to bond with them again. They will love you, Thunder! I will send them a message to announce our arrival."

Thunder interjected, "But what about the hostiles? Will we be safe to travel?"

Uneek replied, "I received an update from the CCL a couple nights ago, stating that the intergalactic community hasn't encountered any hostile forces for quite some time. They were asking for information on their whereabouts. They stated that the universe was suddenly quiet and peaceful. They were completely mystified and confused but were earnestly searching for an explanation from anyone."

"Wow! Wouldn't that be a blessing to have a hostile-free universe!"

Uneek said, "A much needed blessing. So many lost their lives, their home planets, and stellar systems. It would definitely be a blessing if the hostiles were gone forever!"

After a moment of silence, Uneek said, "Eat and drink up. Then we'll be leaving."

Thunder headed for the forest, returning to Uneek in no time. He was ready.

Uneek and Thunder teleported to the Taurus region of the universe. Uneek intermittently switched to cruise control off and on to show Thunder various nebulas with beautiful star clusters. Uneek took his time to show Thunder the beauty of the Crab Nebula. They were nearing the Pleiades, so Uneek messaged ahead that Thunder would need to stay on a hospitable exoplanet while they were visiting. He explained that Thunder was an ancient apatosaurus, requiring food, water, oxygen, and a moderate climate. The Sisters responded almost immediately. They had the perfect planet for Thunder to stay on. They would all meet there. The coordinates were relayed which provided the location of the planet in the Maian star system.

Thunder, being the treasure trove of knowledge on Earth matters, had never experienced anything close to what was transpiring, as he was cruising through the cosmos with Uneek. Thunder was so awe-stricken that he barely spoke a word with the exception of an occasional exclamatory "Ooh!" or "Wow!". Despite his tight-lipped responses, his eyes told it all, big as saucers, constantly moving about so as not to miss a thing. This was a unique experience that Thunder could add to his immense collection of special knowledge. As they rounded the Crab Nebula, Uneek teleported to the Pleiades and the designated planet Draytrea.

CHAPTER 55
MAIA

Maia and her entourage of siblings welcomed Uneek and Thunder with open beams. They had all minimized their magnitudes to small sparks of star light, in the same way that Uneek did. Draytrea proved to be the perfect planetary "hotel" for Thunder. It was the ultimate goldilocks world, vibrant and teeming with every life form imaginable. The plant life was far more advanced than that on Earth. The flora had evolved beyond mere flowering angiosperms, but had diversified into millions of species of beautiful, mobile plants. They could be seen moving around everywhere in the dense forests and meadows. The ecosystem of Draytrea was conducive to the eventual development of smart plants, able to move like animals. The life enhancing climate and environment, over millions of years, gave rise to a plethora of diversification. Some plants and animals converged into one species. New forms of life, organisms consisting of a special combination of both evolved. The beauty of these hybrid species was astonishing and awe-inspiring.

The fruits and nuts were extraordinarily huge. The birds, insects, and peculiar animals coexisted peacefully in harmony with each other. Pollution was nonexistent, as was aggression. The climate was consistently warm and humid with no changing seasons. Both the air and water were pure. There was no marked distinction between day and night like on Earth, because Draytrea received overlapping starlight from a trinary star system. Both Thunder and Uneek were pleasantly surprised by the Sisters' planetary selection.

Excusing himself from the crowd, Thunder headed toward an enticing field of colorful vegetation. He had to test out the new flavors that Draytrea offered. Uneek explained to the Sisters that despite his size, Thunder was shy. The situation was probably a little overwhelming to him, so he left to find solace in whatever comfort food he could find. Uneek told them that Thunder would warm up to them given a little time. He shared Thunder's story with the Sisters who were very understanding of his plight. Maia told Uneek that all of them had experienced a sense of love and warmth emanating from Thunder's spirit despite his timidity. They were sure that the spiritual bonding with Thunder would come in time. Uneek also told them that Thunder could be moody and cantankerous at times. Maia spoke up, "Of course! That is understandable with what he's been through. His beautiful spirit shines through it all, and we sense it."

Electra spoke up then. "We recently received a message from the CCL stating that the hostiles had mysteriously disappeared, and that they were unable to find any trace of the hostiles. They were asking for information on their possible whereabouts."

Uneek said, "Yes. I received the identical message."

Electra said, "The last we heard about them was relayed in a warning from the CCL that hostile forces were seen heading to our sector of Taurus. We prepared ourselves for possible warfare, but nothing ever happened. It was strange, though. We did witness a huge light flash in the Hyades star cluster. It happened so quickly that if you weren't looking in that direction at that time, you would have missed it! Only three of us saw it. Taygete, Alcyone, and I were searching the cosmos for possible areas that the hostiles may approach from, when the flash occurred. We talked about it for a long time and decided it was probably just a new starburst or an implosion. They happen all the time in nebulae."

Thunder could be seen in the distance slowly making his way back to the group. His body was wrenching, and he was spitting profusely everywhere, snorting loudly with disgust.

Maia asked him, "What's wrong? You don't like Draytrean flora?"

Thunder replied stuttering, "Oh no. I mean oh yes! The plants, fruits and nuts are the most flavorful flora that I have ever eaten! But the fauna, not so much. I saw a beautiful flower that I thought I wanted to try. It looked so appetizing. I reached out my neck, plucked it off of the trunk of a tree with my mouth, and began chomping on it. I spit it right back out. It burst in my mouth, oozing some nasty, bitter fluid as I clamped down on it! It was an animal! I know it! I spit up for a full half hour, trying to get that awful taste out of my mouth! I must have drunk 20 gallons of water from the creek!"

"What color was it?", Maia asked.

"It was orange with blue and green spots, and it was shaped like a flower."

The Sisters started laughing in unison, embarrassing Thunder, whose cheeks had turned bright pink.

"You ate a lapitroll!"

Thunder asked, "What is that?"

"It is a small animal that has evolved into a well-disguised flower. They attract smaller animals and insects which they eat. You can see them perched on tree trunks throughout the woods. They are known for their acidic, bitter taste, but fortunately, they are not poisonous."

Thunder turned his head away from the group and snorted several times, intermittently gagging with utter revulsion.

Uneek spoke up. "Thank you for turning your head before snorting!" Addressing the Sisters, Uneek added, "You don't ever want to be in the line of fire when it comes to Thunder's snorts. The discharges will make you sizzle and smoke!" They all laughed jovially, and even Thunder joined in, still red-faced.

The evening was spent exchanging small talk and niceties. Every so often the group would break out in a burst of hilarious laughter. Thunder melded in with all the Sisters, who provided warmth from their glowing light. They partied into the wee hours of the Draytrean morning, bonding in spirit, heart, and soul. They were all uplifted, transcending to higher levels of being.

Thunder began to peter out, his attention span diminished, and his eyelids drooped heavily covering his huge eyes. He had seen so much along the journey here. He had seen galaxies, star clusters, and the vast darkness of the cosmos in-between. Their images kept dancing around in his head. Every so often an orange, blue, and green spotted flower crept into his thoughts, which he immediately shooed away, like an unfriendly spirit. He and Uneek had traveled over 400 light years, and he was tired. Thunder forced himself to rouse enough to get a drink of water before retiring. Even though it wasn't needed, Uneek started a fire to keep Thunder warm after the Sisters left, taking their warm glows with them. Thunder thanked the Sisters for their endearing hospitality. Before leaving, Uneek and the Sisters started humming the familiar song that Thunder had heard so many times before. He joined in the ritual as best he could and soon was hummed asleep.

The small fire blazed, and before the Sisters departed, Uneek told them that he had a couple of earnest things he needed to discuss with them, but that they could wait until tomorrow. They said their goodbyes, and Uneek thanked them all for having them. Wishing each other a good might, the Sisters left. Uneek beamed with joy. Seeing the Sisters always made him happy.

Chapter 56
Turning the Key

Thunder and Uneek were awakened by the most beautiful harmonizing they had ever heard in their lives. The Seven Sisters were a short distance away in the forest singing. Uneek and Thunder found them gathered in a circle, elevating their spirits in melodious vibrations. The song they were singing was different from the tune Uneek was familiar with.

As they carefully approached so as not to disturb the Sisters' ceremony, Uneek and Thunder were welcomed with exuberant smiles and heartwarming light beams. The Sisters made room for Uneek to enter the circle and join in, while Thunder moved in as close as possible. Before long, they were all singing and humming together. Their individual sounds melted together as the new, varied spectrum of changing chords gradually culminated in a euphoric crescendo. The experience was exhilarating, as their hearts and souls united, transcending to the highest states of pure love and ecstasy. Uneek glanced behind him at Thunder whose face shone brightly with an aura of peaceful contentment as he hummed along with eyes closed. Uneek had never seen Thunder this way. He was beaming with love.

Slowly, the singing lowered to a hum, becoming fainter and fainter, fading into eventual silence. The quiet peace that they all felt filled their souls. They had become one with their surroundings and with each other. Thunder opened his eyes and looked around at the others, dying to say something. He couldn't hold in his emotions any longer and said, "Thank you all so much. That was refreshing. I am so happy that you let me join in."

Maia replied, "You are one with us now. Our bond has been sealed in spirit and in love forever." Uneek and all the other Sisters nodded in agreement, expressing the same sentiment.

Looking at Uneek and Thunder, Electra said, "We do this every morning to start our day. We are so glad that you could join us."

Thunder humbly said, "I haven't felt such joy for eons! Thank you." He slowly got up off of the ground. "Excuse me, please. I'm getting a little hungry. I have to eat."

Maia chuckled saying, "Be careful what you put in your mouth!" The group burst out in jovial giggles. Thunder walked away, laughing to himself. Watching Thunder leave, Alcyone said, "He is absolutely adorable! Where in the world did you find him? What a gem of a soul!"

Uneek said, "Yes. He is definitely special."

As the vibrations in his soul lingered on, Uneek decided this was a good time to address the Sisters. He explained in detail the actual problem confronting him in regard to releasing Thunder from the warp.

Maia thought hard and said, "A mile underground?"

Uneek replied, "Yes, unfortunately. I can't imagine how to get Thunder there."

All the Sisters started deliberating amongst themselves. After what seemed to be an eternity, Alcyone finally suggested, "How about time traveling back into the past? You should be able to locate the exact spot when it was at sea level, before all the geological changes took place."

Uneek was dumbfounded! He immediately accessed the control panel and its many options presented in his mind. The Sisters waited patiently in silence, anxiously watching him.

Maia said, "Go to the 'Travel' option."

Uneek explored the 'Travel' option, finding teleportation and continued to look further into levels he hadn't seen before. There it was! 'Time Travel'! He searched the sublevels, finding time regression and time progression. From the surprised look on his face, the Sisters could tell that he had found it.

Uneek exclaimed out loud, "I had no idea!"

CHAPTER 57
THE SEVEN SISTERS HELP

Uneek spent several days learning the particulars of time traveling, that he hadn't previously known he possessed. He made several short trips, both into the past and the future, just to test it out. He would be able to perfect this ability after returning to Earth. He was exasperated by his own stupidity. He should have figured this out on his own. He finally came to the conclusion that two or more minds can be better than one. Afterall, what are friends for? And the Sisters were truly his friends.

Uneek felt indebted to the Sisters for more than just their problem solving. They were wise beyond belief. They had welcomed his best friend with sincere openness and love, and even bonded with him. Thunder was on cloud nine ever since. Uneek had never seen him so happy. He sang and hummed all of the time now. The Sisters had been very generous to him and Thunder. Uneek didn't want them to think he was ungrateful, or that he was taking advantage of their love and kindness. They had helped him out in so many ways already, and he would be eternally thankful. With a little hesitation, Uneek spoke to the Sisters about possibly coming to Earth. He had a plan. He explained the dire situation that existed on Earth. He wanted the Sisters to help raise the spiritual awareness and consciousness of Earthlings. Uneek imagined the Sisters surrounding the entire planet and singing their beautiful songs for all humanity. The beautiful vibrations would touch all souls, lifting them up to places they'd never experienced before. Maybe this would make a difference. It was worth a try. Was this too much to ask?

The Sisters were instantly amenable to the idea. Uneek's heart throbbed with enthusiasm. His mind blazed with anticipation. His soul knew that Earthlings needed guidance. Too many had suffered for too long. The situation was desperate, and the empty void in their souls needed to be filled with love and enlightenment in order to restore hope and faith.

Thunder was delighted with the idea, too. The Seven Sisters decided to accompany Uneek and Thunder back to Earth to wield their magical powers of song.

During the return to Earth, the Sisters paused several times to show Uneek and Thunder some of their most beloved star systems. The Sisters explained that many stars in these systems provided solar energy and light to numerous planets, where highly evolved civilizations lived and thrived. They also passed slowly through the sector where a new, massive supply complex was being constructed to support the needs of these benevolent civilizations. The CCL was busy overseeing the 'Resurrection Project', establishing supply outlets throughout the universe. The combined efforts of stellar civilizations in their construction united them with purpose and meaningful employment. New learning centers were also popping up to provide educational needs and house the priceless knowledge of the cosmos in magnificent libraries, accessible to all.

There was much work to be done. The less fortunate needed to be attended to. Civilizations in unstable systems required assistance in relocating to more favorable cosmic environments. Disease, plagues, and natural catastrophes were a constant in the ever-changing universe. The scope of problems was overwhelming to behold, but with perseverance and dedication, the natural progression of all life would be supported and maintained by the continuing efforts of selfless, conscientious beings throughout the universe. Life was slowly returning to normal again, and the damage that evil beings had caused was being repaired. The memory of the hostiles and their dark agenda was fading away and was being replaced by the light of more powerful forces of love of life.

The trip back to Earth was enlightening not only to Thunder, but even more so to Uneek. The Sisters' informative explanations of sites that were shown to him, provided a valuable update on some of the recovery efforts being undertaken. He was elated and joyful, seeing the positive progress of the 'Resurrection Project'. He felt reassured that his decision to act in defiance of CCL guidelines, had been the correct move to make. The results of his actions were evident everywhere, as the cosmic community rebuilt itself. Uneek smiled to himself.

The small band of travelers was nearing the outer realms of the Milky Way Galaxy, where the beautiful, blue planet rotated on its axis and revolved around the Sun star. A strange feeling stirred within Uneek's soul. He was returning Thunder to his home, along with an entourage of stunning, blue stars, who would assist him in carrying out the next step in his plan, the resurrection of Earth.

Chapter 58

Resurrection

Uneek and Thunder teleported back to the Navajo Reservoir and their campsite. Thunder spent the next few days enjoying the warmth of the lake water and basking in the sunshine.

Uneek watched the Seven Sisters position themselves around the Earth. They had reduced their energy output to safe levels. They surrounded Earth at strategic locations in order to achieve optimum acoustic effects. Pulsating in unison, the Sisters began emitting subtle streams of vibrating energy. Calming sounds enveloped the entire blue sphere. Uneek heard the faint chorus of melody that was generated. The brilliant symphony permeated the atmosphere of Earth, raising the eyes of millions of astonished onlookers. As their beautiful song reached undulating crescendos, the music became audible around the world, drawing the attention of millions in cities and towns, in fields, in forests, and in hills and valleys. Human activity abruptly halted, as people gathered to watch and listen to the sparkling stars in the sky. Dogs barked and whined, wolves howled, cats meowed, cows stood perfectly still, and whales in the oceans sang along in deep, reverberating tones. Even plants responded to the vibrations.

Once the initial shock of the alien presence wore off, people gradually surrendered to the captivating beauty of the song, swaying arm in arm. The long-awaited time of alien disclosure was finally revealed to the masses. The consciousness of the entire planet was awakened. People scurried out of buildings and vehicles stopped in the middle of highways to get a glimpse of the shining Sisters. Some in the crowds of Earthlings sang and hummed in unison, while others remained silent in disbelief and deep reflection. It was as if they inherently knew and recognized the meaning of the phenomenon. Spirits were lifted, as they experienced the higher levels of awareness of the interconnectivity of all life on Earth and in the heavens. This was occurring across continents around the world. Many had prayed for this day, believing all along. This was the day of baring souls, the day of reckoning. In these moments, despair was replaced by hope and joy, and isolation gave way to peaceful, social communion. Pain and suffering were momentarily forgotten. Some were fearful. Most were fearless. Many cried out openly, celebrating with utmost joy. Some were quietly suspicious, stubbornly disbelieving and denying the validity of the cosmic event which was occurring right before their ears and eyes.

This was a moment for the unification of souls, and what it meant to be truly human. Their innate, subconscious connection to the universe was awakened. They were released from their prisons of fallacious belief systems by an external force, as they all beheld the awesome spectacle before them. This shocking realization was made more palpable by the gentle, rhythmic vibrations pouring forth from the Seven Sisters. Like beacons of light, the stars pulsated and sang their way into the deepest part of humanity's collective soul, saying, "We are the Seven Sisters of the Pleiades. We come in peace. We love you and will guide you as you make your way through life and venture into the cosmos. Remember this day, what you feel and what you've realized to be true. We will always be here to help you. Never give up hope, never lose your faith, and never stop loving one another."

The Sisters began spinning around the planet as their individual voices coalesced into one voice. Their combined chords were elevated to a magnificent crescendo which soothingly touched the psyches of every life form on Earth. Then the peaceful, joyful melody gradually and gently decreased in intensity and subsided, leaving Earth in a heightened sense of awareness and sacred enlightenment.

Uneek thanked the Sisters for their wonderful presentation before they left. Thunder was brimming with inspiration and hope for humanity. He was humbly grateful to the Sisters for sharing their wisdom with Earthlings. He conveyed his deepest respect and love for them through the eternal bond they had forged. The Sisters were happy with the receptivity of the majority of Earthlings and left Earth with a joyous song. "You are all welcome. We are glad we could help."

Uttering to himself in his usual, private manner, Thunder said, "Maybe now humans will realize that there are greater forces at play than being asininely stuck up each others' derrieres!" Uneek smiled to himself, thinking Thunder was still the condescending grump, but fully understood why. Despite his uncouth, crude selection of words, his disdain for some Earthlings and their self-induced plight was clear. Thunder's communication skills were not particularly refined. He said things as he felt them and as they were without undue politeness or reservation. He was an amorous brute, and as Alcyone had described him, "Absolutely adorable!"

Chapter 59

Time Travel

The sky above was flickering like a strobe light. The ground beneath heaved up and down. Mountains rose and fell away back into the depths of Earth's crust. Volcanoes sunk, rose, erupted and sunk again into Earth's mantle. Rivers, seas, mud, and glaciers flowed and then receded. The landscape sped by like the winds of a cosmic cyclone. The positions of stars and constellations moved in the sky as the millennia passed by faster and faster. The entire cosmos changed its face. Plate tectonics hoisted the land masses upward and then instantly collapsed again with ear shattering rumbles and intense quaking from deep within the ground. One second there were huge expanses of ocean and sea, and in the next, they were gone. Only a blur hinted at the changing seasons. Glaciers appeared and receded again, giving way to flashing greenery.

Encapsulated in a secure bubble, Uneek and Thunder were time traveling into the past at 5 million years per minute. They could have reached their destination instantly, but Uneek wanted Thunder to see and experience the astounding geological changes that had occurred during the past 66 million years. He had provided Thunder with a front row seat of the panoramic view. It was all very interesting and educational to Uneek, even if it was in reverse.

After a gigantic drop of over 1,000 feet, Uneek quickly checked his barometric altimeter readings. They were at 2,000 feet above sea level now and still dropping. The ground shook at intervals as plates realigned themselves again and the pressures underneath the earth's crust increased and decreased. The atmospheric pressure was increasing, as they lost altitude. Thunder winced, opening his mouth wide until his ears popped and the pressure in his eardrums equalized. His eyes were huge, staring in amazement as time and landscape changes whizzed by.

They were regressing in time so fast that their view became indistinctly hazy, like a powerful whirlwind. Uneek watched the time regression very closely now. It was the early Paleocene epoch 59 million years ago, and soon they would be reaching the late Cretaceous Era. They had dropped another 1,500 feet. At 500 feet above sea level and nearing the end of the Cretaceous Period, Uneek recalibrated the time travel system, decreasing the speed of regression. Instantly, the landscape became less hazy and more distinct. The land was barren, a dead black and brown, like everything had been scorched. There were no plants or animals to be seen. No dinosaurs. No life. Suddenly the sky darkened, heavy with dust and volcanic ash clouds. Magma sputtered forth from beneath the ground and rose high into the atmosphere, covering the lands with tons of volcanic ash and debris. Fires incinerated all that existed on the earth. A powerful tsunami spread out in all directions, wave after wave, washing away all that lay in its path. Then the asteroid impacted with such a tremendous force that the entire planet was jolted. In the next instant, beautiful blue seawater basins appeared, and flashes of verdant vegetation returned once again. With his exceptional vision, Uneek could see gigantic dinosaurs and other wildlife moving about everywhere. Thunder couldn't see this.

Suddenly they came to an abrupt halt on a small, green-covered hillside, surrounded by a shallow sea. They were at 200 feet above sea level, and the time registered 66,025,169 million years in the past. The entire duration of time traveled had only taken them a little over 18 minutes. Uneek removed the encapsulating, protective bubble around them. He left the cloaking mechanism engaged. He glanced over at Thunder whose eyes were shut, his body shaking. He grimaced, slowly opening his eyes, and sighed heavily. He exhaled with a deep groan and said, "Phew! That was intense! The visuals were amazing, but they were frightening and made me kind of sick to my stomach and a little dizzy."

Uneek immediately asked, "Are you okay? I didn't realize you were having any problems. How do you feel now that we are here?"

"Like my guts just got turned inside out!", Thunder replied emphatically.

Uneek noticed Thunder was still trembling. He didn't know whether it was from fear, shock, or the intense ordeal they had just been through. He just exclaimed, "We're finally here!"

Thunder looked around slowly scrutinizing his surroundings. He regained some semblance of his normal senses and bearings. Uneek said excitedly, "This is your home, Thunder! We're here! We made it back to your birthplace! Your old stomping grounds! What do you think, buddy?"

"I think I'm a little sick, but thirsty!", Thunder snorted. He walked down to the edge of the bank to take a drink from the sea and quickly spat the water back out again. He complained loudly, "That's some nasty water! Salt water! Yuk!"

"That's part of the Western Interior Seaway that you just took a drink from," Uneek said. He found a freshwater stream nearby where Thunder could quench his thirst. He drank for a long, steady while.

Looking up, Thunder added, "And I think I'm hungry!" He stared longingly at a group of plants growing along the stream as if he was trying to discern what they were. Finally his memory clicked in and with a loud burst of enthusiasm, he bellowed, "Cycads! Conifers! Hungus plants, merry berries, fern trees, gigantic mushrooms and fungi!" He hastened his steps and swiftly strolled over to indulge in the familiar delicacies of his prehistoric past. Uneek was not surprised by Thunder's inability to grasp the full extent of his whereabouts or what the implications were. He was eating which served as a great stress reliever. He was probably battling the reality of being back home by internally ignoring it. Everything had happened so fast that he had little time to absorb it all. Evening was drawing near. Uneek would have time to talk to Thunder and explain the true meaning of this very important point in time.

Uneek zeroed in on the location of the beacon. It signaled from about 100 yards away and was on ground level, not over a mile below ground. They were still in New Mexico, but in a different era, a different time. He had also noticed that Thunder's time warp had disappeared! He was alive now before he was placed in the time warp. As Uneek gazed up at the heavens with his telescopic vision, he noticed a blazing light in the distant, night sky. It was heading straight toward Earth. This was the immense asteroid! Uneek assessed it to be over 6 miles in diameter! Impact would occur in 31 hours!

CHAPTER 60
BITTERSWEET FREEDOM

After spending the entire day exploring and reacclimating to his former habitat, Thunder meandered lazily back to the camp that Uneek had hastily set up for them. He was anxiously waiting to talk to Thunder about the next steps in his plan. Peering up at the incoming asteroid, he noticed an area in the star-studded sky that was completely dark, blocking out the stars shining behind it. Uneek felt an eerie and ominous foreboding as he studied it. Was this entity the perpetrator of the time warp? Suddenly, Uneek was overcome by an extreme sense of fear, realizing that his suspicions were correct. Uneek quickly got Thunder's attention and explained that they had to leave immediately.

"But we just arrived here! I like it here!", Thunder said with frustration.

"Thunder! Trust me! We have to leave now!" Uneek didn't have time to explain any more to Thunder. He secured the protective bubble around Thunder and himself, hastily set the time progression coordinates, and engaged the time travel system. Within seconds, he and Thunder reappeared back in the Badlands of New Mexico! There was no watching the progression of Earth changes this time around. In a flash, they had traveled from the prehistoric past to the present. This time, Thunder had no side effects, but he was not a happy camper.

"Uneek! What in the world did you do! You whiz me around from place to place, from one time to another, like I'm one of your toy projects!"

"I didn't have time to explain! I spotted the dark entity, and it was preparing to put you back into the time warp!"

Thunder fell completely silent at hearing this, desperately trying to understand the meaning and implications of Uneek's imperative words and actions. In deep thought, Thunder gradually realized what had happened and why. He just said, "I get it." He went silent again, realizing what could have happened to him again.

"Thunder, the time warp is finally gone. You are free now."

"I know. Can we go back to our camp at the lake? I don't care for these badlands at all."

"Sure," Uneek replied and teleported them back to the Navajo Reservoir.

Uneek could feel Thunder's pensive sadness and melancholy mood. They both understood the consequences of what freedom from the time warp actually meant. Thunder would finally be able to move on in his life's natural progression and be able to die. They didn't talk openly about what the future on Earth held for Thunder, but they both knew deep inside. Thunder realized the inevitable was fast approaching, and his spirits were profoundly depressed. Uneek tried to remain cheerful despite his friend's despondency and his own sadness. In an attempt to lighten the mood, Uneek asked, "How about if we camp out in the desert tonight under the stars and have a long heart to heart talk like we usually do?"

Thunder replied unenthusiastically, "Okay." He sounded so sad and dejected.

Uneek realized how difficult this was going to be. In fact, the most difficult time in his entire life was getting ready to unfold. He noticed that Thunder was aging quickly. The whiskers on his muzzle had turned grayish white and his body seemed to be shrinking right before his eyes. Uneek teleported with Thunder to a secluded area of beautiful desert land surrounded by ancient rock formations. Tumbleweeds rolled past them haphazardly like spiked balls, blown by the gentle desert breeze. Uneek started a campfire, and Thunder cuddled close to it for warmth. The desert nights were chilly.

Thunder said inquisitively, "Do you think there's an afterlife?" He desperately sought Uneek's opinion. He sat up. and looked into the heavens as if imploring them for an answer. "Do you think this is all there is and then nothing?"

Uneek came closer to Thunder, and they both stared into deep space. "I think our spirits continue to exist after they leave our bodies," Uneek said. "They return to where they came from."

"Will I see Ella and my children there? My friends?"

"You will see everyone and everything," Uneek said. "It is the inevitable destiny of us all. We are all part of nature's process of life and death."

For the first time in hours, Thunder laughed and said, "I always say, 'I'll be dead a lot longer than I've ever been alive!' That means I'll have to be dead for over 66 million years just to break even!"

Uneek just smiled. He pointed to the sky, showing Thunder the Heart and Soul Nebulas in the Cassiopeian Constellation. "These nebulas are about 7,500 light years away. They are two of my favorites. To me, they represent the link of heart and soul, of life and death. They exist together, and the enlightened spirit can't have one without the other. The heart soul is the highest form of the spirit, and it is infinite."

Thunder sighed, "That is beautiful. All life has a soul, but to live with love, too… that is the ultimate."

"Yes. We are born with their perfect union. Bad experiences during life can sometimes tear the heart and soul asunder. But it is our purpose to pull them back together and keep them united as we live and die. They both go on together in the spirit as the change comes. There is great healing here and there," Uneek responded.

"I'm getting tired," Thunder said, and he moaned with exhaustion.

"Well. That's understandable," Uneek replied. "We've had a long, busy day."

"No. I mean, I'm getting really tired, and I hurt inside and out." Uneek looked at Thunder. His face was gaunter and more wrinkled than when he saw it last.

"Let me put some more wood on the fire, and then we will call it a night. You'll be warm and cozy while you sleep tonight." Uneek stoked the fire, and it blazed, emitting heat against the cold. "Good night and try to think good thoughts. I'll be right here next to you if you need or want anything. I'll see you in the morning. Sleep well and peacefully, my friend."

Thunder replied, "Good night to you, too, my friend. Thank you for everything and all you've done for me. I'll never forget it." He went silent, closing those big, adorable eyes.

Uneek lay, restlessly longing for the presence of his friends, the Seven Sisters. He hummed some of their beloved songs, falling asleep to his favorite tune, the most peaceful lullaby which he had never heard.

The spirits of Gaia, the Pleiadians, Ella, their children Harold and Patty, and the Great Spirit were all present, listening from afar. Even Bright Wolf and Barb heard the lullaby in the midst of their dream states. Many other friendly spirits gathered around in sublime silence, waiting to welcome Thunder as nature took its course.

Chapter 61
Thunder's Passing

The Sun rose slowly above the horizon, spreading rays of star light across the sandy, desert floor. Uneek had not sleep well, tossing and turning all night in unsettling anguish and confusion. He woke early, his mind still foggy. He gazed around and focused unconsciously on the smoldering embers of what remained of the campfire. His mind slowly gathered itself as mental patterns regained shape and meaning. Suddenly, he was overcome by a tremendous sense of dread when his full memory returned. Reluctantly, fighting the inevitable, he looked at Thunder. He was still lying next to him in the same place when sleep had overtaken him the night before. There was no steady heaving of his chest as he breathed. He would have given anything to hear him snore, but Thunder lay perfectly motionless. Uneek sharply perceived that Thunder was no longer in his body which had now shriveled to half its normal size. He was literally disintegrating. When the realization of Thunder's passing became clear, Uneek let out a tremendous wail which emanated from the deepest part of his soul.

He threw himself over Thunder's cold neck and sobbed. Uneek's grief consumed him, and his heart splintered into a million burning embers. He had never felt anything like this in his life. He lay draped like this for a long time, releasing all his emotions until he went numb with emptiness. Thunder eventually disappeared underneath him. Uneek found himself lying in a great depression left by Thunder's massive body. He slowly moved up and out of the deep pit.

Uneek's essence as a bright, shining star had imploded like a black hole, leaving a painful, dark void. Time had lapsed like a stealthy shadow. As Uneek regained clarity of his surroundings, he became aware of the intense midday sunlight which filled his empty, hurting soul, rendering little comfort with its warmth and brightness. As he hovered unsteadily above Thunder's huge imprint, he suddenly became aware of other smaller depressions in the sand. Uneek faintly remembered the night before as if in a dream. They had all appeared to be with Thunder as he passed. As hard as he tried, Uneek could not identify a single print, nor could he recall who they were. Their presence and identity would remain a secret.

Uneek gradually found the energy to deal with the depression he felt and resolved to rely on understanding Thunder's death and death in general. He reached for consolation beyond his own mind. His faith brought a sense of peace back to his mind. So this was the painful price of life when death takes away your loved ones. He knew that all things change and must pass, but this would take a leap of faith he had never known. He felt like the Great Spirit was revealing the truths of life, love, and death. He had become accustomed to Thunder and his friendship, forgetting that it was only temporary, like everything else. Where he had gone, Uneek didn't know, but he could somehow feel Thunder's presence everywhere. He reconciled himself to his own destiny and purpose. He realized that he would have to go on alone. He could hear Thunder saying, "Get over it. I'm okay. I'm still here, just in a different way. That big, old body that I left behind was a pain anyway. Always hungry, thirsty. Either too hot or too cold and slow as molasses. This feels so much better. I'm finally free!"

CHAPTER 62

LEANDRAX

After several days of self reflection and acceptance, Uneek was ready to resume his journey west. He left New Mexico and teleported to Arizona. He levitated for a long time over the Grand Canyon, traveling from slope to slope. The views of its spectacular, historical geology fascinated him. He then headed south to Sedona. He was interested in reaping the benefits of its natural vortexes, and their healing properties. He never envisioned he would be doing this without his friend and traveling companion. Thunder would have enjoyed experiencing the subtle, uplifting energies and power, too. The vortexes would provide much needed sustenance for his grief-stricken heart and empty soul.

Now that Thunder had moved on, Uneek had some unfinished business to take care of. He traveled back in time to confront the dark star. Instantaneously, Uneek appeared in the prehistoric sky. The asteroid had already plunged into the Yucatan peninsula.

He caught sight of the dark star, looming in the distance above Earth. Uneek cautiously approached the star and implored it to identify itself.

The dark star was surprised to encounter Uneek and immediately said, "I am called Leandrax. And you?"

Uneek replied by stating his name and then explained, "You suspended my friend in a space time warp! He suffered for 66 million years trapped by you, until I was finally able to free him from the warp's heinous grip. What did he ever do to deserve such a wicked act?" It took everything in Uneek's power to refrain from blowing the dark star to smithereens.

Leandrax looked shocked and said, "What? What are you talking about?"

Uneek replied, "My friend Thunder! He was an apatosaurus that you caged with your evil technology!"

"But my attempt at saving the dinosaurs malfunctioned. Sadly, they perished!", Leandrax explained with a deep sense of remorse.

"Not Thunder! Your evil act worked on him. I should just blow you out of existence right here and now!", Uneek threatened.

"Wait! Are you telling me that one of the dinosaurs was actually saved? Thunder, you say? I wasn't aware that I put him in a space time warp. I thought it was a complete failure across the board! That means the technology does work, even though it was faulty!"

Uneek screamed at Leandrax, "Well, you definitely failed my friend Thunder!"

Leandrax suddenly became somber and said apologetically, "I had no idea that I entrapped anyone. I watched as the asteroid impacted Earth. It was horrific seeing the devastation, widespread suffering and extinction of almost all plant and animal life. My plan was to save as many dinosaurs as possible! I deployed a space time warp to separate and protect them. I intended to teleport all of them to another planet with a similar habitat. There they could live and thrive and be saved! I had no idea that your friend Thunder got caught in the warp! If I had known, I would have saved him and released him on the new planet!"

Uneek began to understand what had happened. He asked Leandrax, "So, what went wrong with your technology?"

"On my way to Earth, I got hit by a huge solar flare that emitted a tremendous electromagnetic charge. It must have disrupted the system's entire space time warp functionality. If this is true and just one dinosaur was saved, then this means the targeted scope of the area to warp malfunctioned! I could have recalibrated the entire system after replacing a few burned out parts, but by then, it was too late.

"You are from the future, aren't you? I can tell." Leandrax pondered. "How did you get here?"

"Time travel," Uneek explained.

They both looked at one another in bewilderment and disbelief. Then, almost simultaneously, they realized it wasn't too late after all! Leantax could fix his system, and they could travel back in time to reimplement the salvation plan.

Uneek rethought the entire scenario. Thunder's eons of long-suffering entrapment would not have been in vain. Kismet had brought the three lives of Thunder, Uneek, and Leandrax together, and along with many other factors, a new world of living, breathing dinosaurs would be created! A world that would become known as "Thunder World"! Uneek's experience reinforced one of his most valuable tenets. "Leave no stone unturned."

CHAPTER 63
THE TIME FOR HEALING

Considering the turmoil that had raged through Uneek's mind the night before, he awoke with a new perspective and a peaceful demeanor. He realized that constant change was the way of the universe. He embraced the unpredictability of cosmic events. There were things he could never control and reaffirming his faith in the grand scheme of creation, he found sweet solace.

He decided to venture into the desert to explore the area around Sedona. The landscape that lay before him was amazing.

Early morning sunlight bathed him, as he gazed into the distance. Storms were churning out lightning bolts and flashes, and thunder rumbled above the mountains. He imagined his friend Thunder sending him a telepathic message saying, "I'm doing well, Uneek. Thank you for all you did to help me."

Uneek moved toward a nearby stream and watched heavy raindrops spatter its surface as the storm slowly approached. He was momentarily puzzled to see that it flowed uphill instead of downhill. He must be in one of the many vortexes around Sedona. His soul absorbed the calming energy. Sighing deeply, he turned away to continue on his quest westward. He left the past behind to face his future with renewed exuberance.

As Uneek eagerly explored the beaches of the Pacific Coast, he was amazed at the beautiful, colorful diversity of tropical flora. Uneek thought of Thunder and the heyday

he would have had ingesting the fronds of palm trees and huge ferns. The flowering foliage in this area would have been a delectable treat for him.

The ocean was teeming with marine life. Under the water, rocky canyons of the continental shelf provided a natural playground and protection for more endangered aquatic life forms. After venturing for miles along this scenic route, Uneek came upon an inlet which led to a beautiful, secluded bay. Partially obscured by tall trees and high cliffs, it was situated in a remote area of the coast. Submerged under deep, pristine waters, Uneek saw ridges of sand-covered shoals rising from the ocean floor. Uneek climbed up onto a nearby ridge to peer out at the bay's breathtaking expanse that gave way to the open ocean several miles in the distance. Uneek envisioned Thunder, soaking in the bay. He lifted his head up and out of the water, emerging with a mouthful of dripping, dangling seaweed. Uneek visualized him snorting as he swallowed, spitting out distasteful crabs and oysters. Uneek chuckled to himself at the thought and said to himself, "I miss you, you big, funny brute."

As he sat on the edge of the ridge, a reddish orange crab slowly crawled its way toward him. It only had one claw and struggled to make forward progress. His claw must have been lost during battle. It reminded him of all the hardships that life forms on this planet endured in their individual struggles to survive. Fortunately, in this wonderful environment, the missing claw could regenerate itself, hopefully before it became a victim to another predator.

Uneek felt a tinge of sadness as he weighed the implications of the life and death reality of this strange world. Living here was definitely no easy task for anything or anybody. Survival depended not only on strength, but also on intelligence, and a lot of luck.

CHAPTER 64
DANCE OF THE DOLPHINS

A distant, splashing noise drew Uneek's attention from these deep thoughts to the glistening surface of the bay. Suddenly, a dolphin jumped out of the water, discharging air and water through a blowhole on top of its head. It took in a deep breath as it rose 20 feet into the air, turned, and dove back down, hitting the water with a huge splash. The dolphin had noticed Uneek sitting on the cliff edge as it came back up to the surface and started squeaking signals. In a few minutes, dolphins started jumping in and out of the water everywhere. Their joyful, frolicking display amused Uneek, and any residual feelings of sadness vanished from his heart. The first dolphin must have spread the word, and before long, the entire colony of dolphins put on an impressive show for the unexpected visitor. Uneek saw that the crab had mysteriously disappeared, apparently realizing that this was too much activity and too close for his safety.

The second act of the show soon followed, when the alpha male of the pod stood up on the water! He pumped his tail vigorously, working his flukes underwater to maintain an upright position. Soon all the other dolphins did the same, creating a huge circle of moonwalkers. Uneek was amused by their agility and playfulness. The alpha male turned around several times and the others copied his moves in tandem. Squeaking happily, their bodies twitched with glee as they danced in a swirling frenzy, until the alpha male suddenly stopped. Still buoyant on top of the water, he peered into the distance. He had eaten only a small breakfast that morning, consisting of squid and shrimp, and he was hungry. He had kept an eye out during the entire show, when he suddenly saw a huge, dark shadow under the blue-green water approximately 100 yards away. Having spotted the school of fish, he squeaked, "Over there! Quick! Sound the dinner alarm, Jumper!"

"Will do, Echo! I just hope they aren't anchovies. If they are, I'll have to pass. Cod or herring would be quite tasty right about now!" Using his natural sonar ability, Jumper alerted the rest of the pod. It was dinner time! His skillfully executed alert did not disturb the school of Pacific herring, looming in the distance. The bay area directly in front of Uneek was quickly vacated as one by one, the dolphins disappeared to zero in on their prey. The entertainment was over for now as hunger took precedence.

While the dolphins were gone, Uneek had the chance to find out more about these beautiful creatures. Accessing the archives of Earth life forms, he learned that dolphins were not fish at all, as he had originally suspected. They were warm-blooded and descended from land mammals roughly 50 million years ago. They entered the oceans to live, evolving into whales, dolphins, and porpoises. Dolphins became one of the most highly specialized mammals that exists on Earth. They exuded sound waves in a process of echolocation. The sound waves traveled through the water, bouncing off of objects, which disclosed their location. Dolphin lungs had developed to the point where they could remain underwater for 15 minutes or longer. They were extremely intelligent, as Uneek had discovered by listening to their high-pitched form of communication. He was able to understand their language.

It wasn't long before the dolphins returned, popping in and out of the bay close to him. Satisfied and plump, most were engaged in burping up air and water through their blowholes, wallowing in the shallows. They rolled over and over again, and it was obvious by their bloated underbellies that the feeding went well.

Suddenly, Echo came up from the depths, eyeballing Uneek curiously. He was surprised to see Uneek still resting there on the ridge. Uneek made an attempt to smile in his own special way.

Echo swam closer and hoisted himself up on the edge of the ridge to face Uneek directly. In a high-pitched squeak, Echo introduced himself and then his entire pod, as one by one, each swam to Uneek, exchanging names and greetings. When Jumper came forward, he made a series of chirping-like sounds. Uneek understood and answered, "Oh yes! Your show was really entertaining. I enjoyed watching all of you."

Jumper went on to explain that they would love to show him more of their dance moves later. But for now, they were all too full and needed time to digest the herring in their stomachs.

Echo asked, "Where did you come from? This cove is very secluded, and we rarely get any visitors. What brought you here?"

Uneek replied, "From the East coast, and before then, from there," pointing up at the sky. This place is so beautiful, I had to stop to take it all in."

Echo said, "I knew that or at least suspected it. You look like the lights in the night sky. I figured you were one of them. Where are you headed to?"

Uneek said, "I want to finish exploring the West coast. Then I'll be returning home."

Echo began telling Uneek about their colony. "Before we found this cove, my pod and I migrated for years, traveling many miles in search of food and warm waters. We have made this bay our home. There's no need to migrate any longer for now. We have an endless supply of fish and squid here. The temperature barely fluctuates. There are no other predators here that might endanger our lives. No large fishing nets that kill us. Only an occasional, lone fisherman. No beach parties, no discarded beer cans, liquor bottles, or dangerous plastic litter. No runoff from big industry or fossil fuel companies. We've seen our share of pollution at the hands of humans, when we were migrating. The water here is pristine, the beaches are clean, and the ocean breeze brings in fresh air. All forms of life thrive here. We are very fortunate and comfortable here. It is good to have a home. We hope the humans don't return and find us or worse, decide to build and move in. Then and only then, will we have to migrate somewhere else."

Uneek was alarmed at the awareness and knowledge that Echo possessed.

Echo went on, "Ever since the great celestial event occurred, things have slowly improved everywhere. It seems that the seven stars that visited Earth, singing their uplifting harmonies, touched every living thing on Earth. It was the most glorious transcendent experience for our entire planet. Actually, it is making a big difference in human mentality. They helped make humans aware of the fragility of the natural world we live in and to take care of it, not plunder it. The repercussions of the extraterrestrial encounter helped humans realize that they are not in control, but only a small part of the universe at large. Other more intelligent, off-planet life forms exist.

"Dominion over the Earth does not mean that it belongs solely for humans to do what they wish with it. The original meaning of dominion was lost and perverted through the millennia. Humans changed it to mean dominance. Dominion's original meaning is for humans to be the caretakers of this world, not the controllers or conquerors. The universal concept was handed down to humans by the extraterrestrials as guidance for them." Uneek was pleased that the influence of the Pleidians were taking root on Earth, and that progress towards the planet's well-being was being made.

The conversation between Echo and Uneek was suddenly interrupted by a mysterious, incoming communique. Uneek thanked all the dolphins for sharing a piece of their lives with him. He explained to Echo the urgency of the situation, and that he had to be on his way. He humbly excused himself and abruptly left the dolphin paradise.

CHAPTER 65

THE CALL

The message was not transmitted in the usual form. It was directed straight into Uneek's soul. It was a summons from an unknown, unidentifiable source. He understood that his presence was requested. When Uneek input the coordinates, pointing to the remote origin of the sender, his EUPS could not register a location and indicated no data available. He would be entering a portal that would take him to an undisclosed destination. It was required that he enter the portal corridor in only one dimension, his true dimension. Immediately, Uneek experienced a deep sense of uneasiness. No one knew that he existed in two distinct, but interconnected dimensions simultaneously. He suddenly realized that the source of the message was unbelievably intelligent and knew much more about him than he wanted known. No purpose for the summons was given. The only true grasp he had of this mysterious request was that it required a response and acceptance. He did not hesitate any longer. Shaking with uncertainty, Uneek's soul conveyed acceptance. Instantly, he was swept away.

Uneek could barely remember anything from the whirlwind that ensued. His sense of time and space disappeared, and a sensation of complete emptiness and weightlessness overcame him. He lost hold on reality as he knew it. Everything was stripped from him, and his soul was laid bare and vulnerable. His fate lay in the hands of the summoner, as he bounded toward the celestial realm, the place of souls. His mind raced through time, passing through galaxies, and entire universes.

Traveling through the worm hole was so intense that Uneek lost consciousness.

245

Chapter 66

The Reckoning

As if in a dreamlike trance, a glorious, ethereal castle suddenly appeared before him. It gently drew him into it. Barely aware of his surroundings in the dark recesses of the castle where he found himself, Uneek could make out the sound of a kind voice addressing him. With all-knowing wisdom, it spoke to him.

"I am that which cannot be named. I am called by many names but have none. You have reached out for me many times as you were guided by your faith. I have always been here and always will be for those who are receptive. It was time to finally reveal myself to you.

"Your mission to Earth is coming to an end. You have accomplished preordained milestones and exceeded all expectations. I commend you on your extraordinary achievements.

"You have learned and experienced much: friendship, love, patience, loss, courage, and above all, unwavering faith in the fabric of Creation, my creation. You learned about the affairs of Earthlings, their shortcomings, and the various reasons for them. You have fulfilled your purpose, attaining invaluable knowledge which is vital to the community of infinity. You have proven that Earthlings possess the spiritual potential to be brought into the cosmic arena. Further evolution of their mindsets and belief matrix, along with major changes in current systems, will eventually make this possible. There is hope for humanity after all.

As your mission comes to a close, I want to thank you for your contributions to the furtherance of benevolence. I encourage you to undertake future missions, but it is up to you. All your thoughts and actions were executed with good intentions for goodness' sake, not for yourself, and because of this, you are free. You are a truly special individual. You are Uneek!"

Uneek listened intently but was unable to respond. He could only absorb the words and the blessings.

"I will now return you to Earth so you can say your goodbyes and bring this chapter of your life to a close. One last thing, Uneek. You conducted some nice moves against those who wish to undermine the purpose of my creation. You have restored peace and harmony to this part of the universe, and I commend you for it."

Uneek's self confidence hit an all time high. Some questionable actions he had engaged in were acceptable, and Uneek was actually praised. There was no hiding anything, no secrets left unrevealed. His slate was wiped clean.

"I AM infinity. I exist in everything and am always here. Go forth with good intentions in your heart and soul and keep your mind pure and free."

CHAPTER 67

FULFILLMENT

Uneek floated along above the road. He would miss the beauty of Earth's natural world. No words could describe the exaltation that Uneek felt. One day in the future, he would return to Earth and hopefully find a world in harmonious communion, Earthlings with nature and with each other. It would take time and tremendous upheavals in human psyches. But he had hope for humanity and faith in their ability to overcome evil and adversity.

A sense of loss and loneliness still lingered deep inside of Uneek. He was about to leave this sacred place and head out again into the universe. He was alone and yearned for companionship. Thunder had gifted him with friendship and agape love.

Uneek felt lost as he ascended into the atmosphere, not knowing his destination. He looked back at the blue planet as it grew smaller and smaller. Leaving the Sun system, he was feeling pangs of melancholy, eroding his euphoric sense of happiness. To comfort himself, he started humming one of the Seven Sisters' melodies, which always brought immediate warmth and joy to his aching heart. He knew now where he was headed.

Uneek entered the Pleiadian star cluster unannounced. He was filled with a mixture of both hope and unsurety in anticipation of what he was about to do. The Sisters were all there, and they instantly clustered around him when they became aware of his presence. Laughing with glee, the Sisters welcomed him with enthusiastic warmth.

They began a harmonious melody of happiness. Maia was especially exuberant, her vibrations drowning out those of her Sisters.

"Uneek! What a pleasant surprise! We missed you!"

Uneek said, "I had to come see you. My mission on Earth is complete. It was difficult to leave. I felt so forlorn. I came here, because you always lift my spirits."

"Oh Uneek! We love you and are so happy that you stopped by," Maia replied.

Uneek looked at Maia, his heart light visibly throbbing in his soul. Maia noticed right away and asked, "what's wrong, Uneek? You are vibrating and shining like a pulsar!"

"Nothing's wrong. I'm just excited to see you," Uneek explained shyly.

Maia blushed when she realized he was speaking exclusively to her, and only her. The other Sisters sensed this, and Electra said, "We have something that we need to attend to." They gave space to Uneek and Maia and made a motion for the others to follow her.

Alcyone said, "Maia, you stay here with Uneek and keep him company. We'll be back shortly."

Left alone, Uneek and Maia glanced back and forth at each other. Maia finally said, "You look like you want to say something. You know I love you. What is it, Uneek? We are very close friends, and you can tell me anything. My curiosity is peaking. What is it?"

Then Uneek began timidly. "Maia, I'm a rogue star. I don't want to be alone anymore. I need companionship. I need to exist with someone with whom I can communicate and share my life and experiences. I am drawn to you, Maia. I love you, too."

Maia blushed even deeper at these words. She replied, "You are absolutely magnificent and very special to me."

There was a moment of awkward silence. Then Uneek asked almost reluctantly for fear of rejection, "Would you like to go binary with me?" Waiting for Maia to respond, he blushed for the first time in his life. The anticipation was almost unbearable when he finally heard her soft reply, "Yes, I would."

In the distance they could hear a sudden outburst of gleeful cheers and harmonious shouts of approval. The Sisters had foreseen the outcome of this conjugal exchange. The love shared by Uneek and Maia was obvious to all. The singing Sisters returned and guided the two to a beautiful garden, which they had hastily prepared with elaborate decoration. Uneek embraced Maia as they entered the nuptial garden and engaged in the greatest Pleiadian celebration ever known.

ACKNOWLEDGMENTS

I extend sincere thanks to the following loved ones:

My friend, Denise Brinkley, for your unwavering love and support throughout the years of our friendship. You are always there for me. You are the most patient listener that I have ever met in my life.

Greg Omerzu, my brother, a true kindred spirit with a heart of gold, who always has my back with unconditional love and support.

Elsa Daudert, my maternal grandmother, for her encouragement, support, and unwavering dedication to my upbringing. She inspired me to pursue and develop the gifts and talents I was born with. She taught me to aspire toward the finer things in life, a virtuous spirit, honesty, integrity, and consistency of heart. You always believed and instilled in me an enduring sense of purpose and determination against all odds. Your wisdom, talents and creativity rubbed off on me.

Ruth Omerzu, my mother, for her love, support and the joy expressed whenever she watched me do artwork.

Anton Omerzu, my father, for his love and support of my creative endeavors and teaching me the importance of self discipline.

Wendell Dobyns, my art teacher for 12 years. The most gentle and patient man I was ever blessed to know, who encouraged me throughout my school years.

To my readers:

Katie Reuter,

Wauhnetia (Netia) Mills, and

Fran Milano for your support, time, encouragement, and friendship. Your reactions to my book have been invaluable and much appreciated.

Astrophotographer and microphotographer, Derry Cox, for contributing photos for use in this book: namely, the photos of the Heart and Soul Nebulas, the North American Nebula, and the Vitamin C (Ascorbic acid) crystal.

ABOUT THE AUTHOR

Sonja Ruth Elizabeth Omerzu was born in San Antonio, Texas. She spent her childhood in Fairborn, Ohio, where she exhibited an early interest in art and was gifted with her first set of oil paints at age 5. Sonja's interest in the art world was nurtured by her art teacher of 12 years, Wendel Dobyns. Sonja graduated with honors from Fairborn Baker High School.

Sonja attended Ohio University where in 1972, she received a Bachelor of Arts Degree in English, minoring in philosophy.

Sonja worked simultaneously as a managing salon-owning cosmetologist, as an assistant framing artist, and as an art teacher for Dependent Youth Activities (DYA) at Wright Patterson AFB. In 1984, she became employed by the Defense Logistics Agency, where she specialized in inventory management, retiring from the Defense Supply Center Columbus (DSCC) in Columbus, Ohio after 30 years of service.

Sonja joined Toastmasters while at DSCC to develop her speaking and leadership skills, serving as president, vice president of education, and sergeant at arms. Sonja is a member of American MENSA, a military veteran of the Navy, and the recipient of Bob Ross Certification.

Sonja's hobbies include writing, artwork, reading, and golfing. She is especially interested in nature, animals, extraterrestrial life, extrasensory perception, the prehistoric past, astronomy, metaphysics, music, creativity, enlightenment, constant learning, transcendentalism, self development and actualization, and the social unity of species. She is a strong advocate of human and animal rights.

Sonja adheres to a belief that all things are possible, and that we are so much more than what we are led to believe we are.

Made in the USA
Columbia, SC
11 November 2024

fbf498e8-8c13-49f9-a6d0-32f97d3cc39eR02